SIROUS

OHIO VAMPIRES BOOK 2

KATHI S. BARTON

This is a work of fiction. Names, characters, places, and incidents are products of the author's imagination or are used fictitiously and are not to be construed as real. Any resemblance to actual events, locations, organizations, or persons, living or dead, is entirely coincidental.

World Castle Publishing, LLC
Pensacola, Florida
Copyright © 2025 Kathi S. Barton
Hardback ISBN: 9798275563184
Paperback ISBN: 9798891264960
eBook ISBN: 9798891264977
First Edition World Castle Publishing, LLC, December 8, 2025
http://www.worldcastlepublishing.com
Licensing Notes
Cover: Cover Designs by Karen
Editor: Karen Fuller

Chapter 1

Sirous had everything set up the way that he wanted. He'd arrive at Brew's for a week, where he'd talk to his friends and hang out with them all. After that, he would have his good friend, Yosef, kill him because that was the way that he wanted to go.

He did worry that he'd not be able to remove his head all in one slice, but he had faith in his friend, as they both knew that the sun would no longer kill him if he were caught out in it for an extended period of time. Yosef had agreed to do it long ago, and he wasn't going to allow him to back out of the deal now. However, he did say that if he'd met his mate in the time from now until it was time to kill him, he'd not do it. He was just going to make sure that he didn't meet anyone new for the next two weeks. That should be easy enough, as he'd been around for thousands of years and had never met her, so now wasn't going to be any different.

Most vampires of his age had long since given up on finding their mates. They'd either made arrangements as he'd done to be killed, or they did something that made it so that the council would have to kill them. He preferred his method as he didn't want to linger around waiting for someone to get around to knocking him off. Sirous thought that they'd make it hard on him, too, if he did something that would make them have to kill him. He didn't want a lot of pain, just for it to be over with in record time.

However, he was looking forward to seeing Brew again and his new mate, Cally Lily. She sounded like she was the perfect match to the new king and was looking forward to bowing before him just to piss him off. And it would too, he had no doubt.

He could have willed himself to see Brew, but he wanted to see some things before it was gone from him forever. Like he wanted to see the sun setting over the ocean again, as well as see it rising in the same way. There were places he wanted to say goodbye to as well. Little shops that he'd frequented before that sold candles and good wines. He had invested and invested well in the little shop and was glad to see that it was still striving after all these decades. There were people that he wanted to say goodbye to as well.

All their good friends that he'd made over his lifetime. Yosef was one of many whom he'd like to talk to once more. To see Rutger to play a good game of chess, as well as Rance to just sit and talk about books with one more time. The other, Kenneth, was his best friend, and he didn't care who knew it. But the man had been unlike any other vampire that he'd come across in all his years of roaming the earth.

He often wondered if he had a monster, what all vampires called their other half. Kenneth could charm a woman's favors from her with just a look and a smile. Once when they were out together, he'd lined up three women for his bed, and they all knew about it. Still, they waited their turns and gave him a good time. He was like that. A charmer. And he loved him very much.

Sirous had had enough. He was bored out of his mind with the way things were, and he needed someone to take him to task and remove his head. It was the only way to kill one such as himself, and he was ready and willing to have it done to him. The very least that Yosef could do for him was to remove his head so that he could enjoy the afterlife, if there was one, fully.

As the train he was riding on slowed for another freight train to pass them, he enjoyed his glass of wine and watched the passengers. There were quite a few on board the large train, and he was just as excited to watch them as he was to see the scenery outside the large open windows of the dining car he was in.

He saw the couple that had gotten on board before him enjoying a late supper. He envied them their love — for now at least. Being humans, they didn't know what perils would tear them apart, but he did. Seeing into their future, he knew that in less than one year, the man would cheat on his lovely bride and she would kill him and his lover. But for now, they were happy, and he supposed that was all one could hope for in this world of humans. He looked up when the waitstaff asked him if he was enjoying his trip.

"I am. I'm having a lovely time." He ordered another glass of wine and told the staff member that he wouldn't be partaking of dinner tonight when the others did. Sirous would grab something to eat on the midnight train so that he could enjoy it in peace. Not that anyone on the train was making a lot of noise, but he'd had enough of the humans around him and wanted to catch a nap while they slumbered in their beds. He tipped the young man when he returned with his new glass of red wine.

Sirous could eat should he want to. It wouldn't fill him up like fresh blood did, but he could blend in when necessary. He could also leave the train and return fulfilled, and no one would be the wiser. It was one of the perks he enjoyed at being as old as he was. Again, he was tired of the magic that would get him into trouble at times, like seeing the future of some of the patrons on the train. He didn't tell them, of course, that would just bring unwanted attention to himself.

He knew that the young man who had been

serving him tonight was going to die in ten years. He'd take a lover who wasn't as kind as he was, and he would end up killing the younger man. The woman who changed his bed linens would go on to become a great lawyer in her own right, and she would take on cases that meant the world to others. She would be, with all the others on the ride, the only one who did something productive with her life and lived well beyond her years.

Having contact with so many people on the train gave him a bit of a view on all their futures. Some of them were good lives; most were not. He even knew that the baby that had come on the trip with his parents for some quality time together would become a mass murderer and blame it on his kind parents. They had given him all that he needed, but not what he wanted, and that was everything that he saw. It would take years for them to come to terms with the fact that they'd not been the ones who had caused him to kill women. It has always been in his head that he deserved more than they were giving him, and that's what made him a bigger monster than even Sirous was when he was angry.

As the supper car was being filled with guests, he made his way back to his cabin. It was more than enough for him. Using his considerable magic, he had magically enhanced the room so that while it appeared to be the same size as all the others, he had his own bed as well as a shower and bathroom in his room. He didn't like sharing things like that and was just as happy to make sure that he didn't have to. Pulling down the book he'd been reading, he laid back on his bed and read until the sun had set and the darkness of the night was all there was. Not even a bright star in the sky could invade the darkness that he so loved. He felt someone touch his mind and smiled when he realized that it was Brew.

"Kenneth has arrived and is in good spirits. Though I don't know of a time when he wasn't. He said that he's looking forward to seeing you again after so long." He said that he was looking forward to seeing them all again. *"Yosef told me what your plan is. I've not told my Calla Lily as she will be upset by your plans. However, you will have to tell her yourself when you see her. And hell hath no fury like my mate when she thinks an injustice has occurred. And she will think that when she finds out you wish to have your head removed."*

"I shall tell her what I told you. I'm much too old to be going around doing the same things daily. I've been around longer than her, so I know what I'm about." He thought about asking Brew if he knew that his mate was breeding, but figured that he'd know. Being the king of their kind, he'd have special magic that would be needed to keep her safe now that she was going to

have a child. *"Why do I have the feeling that she is right now lining up a bunch of single women to see if any of them are our mates? Do you suppose that she has any idea how long I've been looking myself? I've given up, my dear friend, and that's the way that I want it."*

"I understand. I wanted the same thing before she came into my life." He said that he was lucky. *"Yes, I am. And I feel so more every day of my life with her around. She is my world and keeps me on my toes daily. I love her."*

"Of course you do." They both laughed. They talked about the others coming to town in much the same manner that he was. Taking their time in coming so that they could see a bit more of the ever-changing world that they all had had a part in creating. *"What of the magic that you have now? Are you stronger than you were before? I'm betting that your mother is very jealous of it all. She's a lovely woman, your mother."*

"She's coming to town as well. In fact, I'm expecting her anytime now. She said that she wanted to get some things from storage to bring to Calla, but she didn't say what she would bring. I can only hope that it's nothing from my childhood. She'd be the only one who could embarrass me like none other." He laughed at the image of Mother Smith bringing out things that Brew had made her when he was no more than a babe. It would do him a world of good to see the big vampire embarrassed, and he told him so. *"Did you know that when I became king, we got*

some faeries that came to the house? I've never seen the like of them. There are quite a few of them around us at all times, but the most important thing is that they're here only to serve us. The household has never been so full before."

"I heard how your lady wife went over your books and found that you were paying a dead woman's family. And quite a few other things you were overpaying for as well. Good for her. If I didn't do my own books, like I told you to do several times in our lives together, I'd be worried as to what she'd find in my books too." He was told how she went over Conri's books and found a great deal of money when the adding had been off by thousands of dollars. *"Good for him. I'm sure that his pack could use it. Are they still looking for work around the town? I've seen in his future that great things are coming his way for himself and his pack."*

"He'll be happy to hear that. I know that I am." He didn't say anything more and was glad that Brew didn't ask him about it. There would be some bad that came with the good news, and he was sure that his friend knew that. *"When can we pick you up? I'm sure that you might have told me, but let me get it straight in my head."*

"I will be at your home in one week. I've some things that I have to take care of once I'm off my trip here, and then I'll be on your doorstep. I'm to understand that you've made some improvements to your home since I was there last. I

will need to be invited in because of the status that you now have."

"You are very welcome, and you know it. Forever if you wish." He didn't take the bait in telling him that he'd not be around forever because he was finished with this world. Instead, he told him that he was looking forward to meeting his mate and seeing their friends again. That was the best he could do under the circumstances. *"I will see you in one week then. And until then, you enjoy your trip. Know too that I love you like a brother and will, no matter what happens."*

He had a moment of worry when it occurred to him that Brew could now order him to live. He might well be planning that, but he doubted that it would come to that. Brew was a good friend and knew the trials of living for so long. He'd been lucky in finding his mate, and he wanted the best in the world for them both. He put his book away in favor of doing one of his errands now and left the train.

There were several investments that he'd made just before deciding that he wanted to die. Looking over the books in the newest adventure, he was satisfied that things were going the way that he thought they should. He couldn't see the futures on things like investments, and it had taken him a long time to get as good as he was with them. But once he decided on something like this little venture, he knew that he'd be making money until the end of time. And leaving everything to Brew as his king, he knew that he'd put his money to good use when the time came. He only hoped that he'd forgive him for leaving things the way that they were and do what he wanted. Some of his money would go to his best friends, and the rest would be for Brew and his lovely new mate, Calla Lily. What a beautiful sounding name.

~*~

Brew watched as Calla put on a robe. He knew her body as well as he did his own and loved every inch of her. They'd made love for the third time today, and he could never get enough of her. As it was now, he was getting very little done in his office because he wanted to spend time with his mate. She turned to look at him as he stared at her fine ass.

"There is more to life than just making love, you know." He asked her if she had enjoyed it. "I came five times, I'm sure you know that I did. Are you fishing for compliments? I have them for you, but I fear it will go to your head and you'll try to outdo yourself. I don't know that I can take much more of your lovemaking than I have right now."

"You love me." She said that she did, with all her heart. "And I love you too, my dearest Calla Lily. Soon you'll be fat with our child, and I'll have to take better care when we make love. No more roughhousing when we get in the mood." She pouted, and he laughed.

"You're perfect for me. I love the way we roughhouse, as you called it. It makes me come all that much harder." He felt his face break out in a large grin. She could do that to him, make him happy with just a word or two. "Your mother will be here soon, and we need to get going to be ready for her. I'm glad that she agreed to stay with us. We certainly have the room for her."

"She'll still think that we're being put out. But she has magic that will change the room should she want to. And I'm sure that she will if only to have a few of her things around her while she's staying here." When she nodded and continued to look out the window, he knew that she was distracted and decided to see what he could get away with while she was. "Sirous is planning to die once he's here. I hope that he'll do it when we're not around while his body will turn to ash."

"That's nice." She turned to look at him. "There is something out there that I can't see." He asked her what she meant. "I can feel a presence, but I can't see them. It's not the wolves. I can feel them and where they are, but this…well, this thing is out there and can't get into the house without an invite. Could it be one of your friends?"

"They'll be your friends soon enough, and let

me see what I can find out." He reached out to the others and asked them if they had arrived. "It's Rutger. He's surprised that you can feel him. He was trying to hide in the event that we were too busy to mess with him right now."

"Does he mean sex?" He nodded. "Well, tell him that it wouldn't matter if he was at the door or not, I'd finish, then come let him in. Come on, get dressed so that we can meet him. Kenneth is in the living room watching something on the television. He'll be happy to see the other vampire."

Brew was happy too to see his old friends and hurried to get dressed. Once he was, he ran down the stairs, picking up Calla as he went, and carried her to the door. Putting her down just as the door opened with his magic, he looked at his friend and nearly burst into tears, much the same way he'd done when Kenneth had arrived several days ago.

"I invite you into my home forever." As soon as he stepped over the threshold, Brew pulled him in for a long hug and hardy embrace while fighting the tears that threatened him a great deal of late. "I've missed you."

"And I you." They hugged tightly for another few minutes, and when they released, they hugged once again. "I want you to meet my wife, Calla Lily Smith. Calla, this is Rutger, one of the few friends that I can count on to come when I want to see them. Rutger, Calla is my queen and best thing that has ever happened to me."

"I can tell." Rutger got down on one knee before Calla. "I pledge to you, my queen, my life and all that goes with it. I shall forever be at your beck and call from now to the end of the ages. You are my queen."

"You're supposed to do that to the king." He said that Brew already had his loyalty, but he wanted her to have his life. "Thank you, Rutger. Hopefully, I'll never need you to lay down your life for me. And in turn, I would do everything within my power to make sure that you're safe and well, as your queen and hopefully friend."

Rutger hugged Calla, and he found that he wasn't jealous at all for her being hugged by another man, much less a vampire. As they separated, he asked about the babe, and it was with a huge grin on her face that she told him that she was going to have a baby in the early spring.

"I just went to the doctor for our kind this morning and found out. He said that I had to eat more food for the baby, but otherwise, I was in good shape to carry it to term. He said that he could tell us what it was, but we already know that it's a boy. I'm so happy to be having Brew's baby that I could about bust." Her charm was infectious, and soon Rutger was gushing about the baby as well.

Calla had that sort of charm to her when she wanted to be. There were times when she'd be so upset that he feared for the other person on the receiving end of her anger. But she was calm and cool when dealing with others, and he loved that about her, too.

So far, they'd only had to deal with one vampire that was in trouble with the laws that govern them, and she'd dealt with it better than he might have. He would have killed the man outright for his misdeeds, but she gave him a second chance to mend his ways. Time would tell if it worked or not, but he had a feeling that the vamp would turn his life around and not be making baby vampires anymore. If he did, then Calla said that she'd deal with him, and she never gave a third chance. Nor would it be a quick death, as she would string it out for days, and he'd be begging for death that might not ever come until she was finished with him. That scared even him just a little.

Kenneth was just as happy to see Rutger as they were. When the three of them were together, they hugged each other again and got a little teary-eyed. It had been far too long since they'd seen each other, and he was glad that they could get together. Friends like his weren't ones that came around in several lifetimes of living. They were the kind that lasted until well beyond death.

His mother arrived just as Calla was sitting down to dinner. The four of them joined her because they got a kick out of the things that she ate. Tonight she was having a burger and French fries with a malted milkshake. Her sucking on the straw had him hard as stone again, and he knew that he had to behave himself or she'd take him to task. He loved it when she got bossy with him and couldn't have been happier when they made love to make up for it, too.

"I've heard that Sirous is planning to kill himself when he arrives." He looked around the table, then back at his mom when she continued. "The poor man has been around for longer than most and hasn't met his mate. What are you going to do about it, son? Allow him to do this thing?"

"I cannot stop him. Oh, I guess I could order him to live, but I won't do that to him." Brew glanced at Calla as her burger stopped between the plate and her mouth. "I told you about it, love. You were distracted, but I did tell you about him wanting to die."

"You tricked me, is what you did." She put down her burger and glared at him. "You'll order him to live, and that's final. Or I will. I'll not have him coming here to off himself when there are plenty of things going around here that can change his mind. If I have to, I'll line up every single and married woman around to see if he can find his mate. He won't be able to do it once he finds her."

"He thought you might do that. He said as much to me." She glared at him again. "I don't want this any more than you do, love. We'll all try to convince him to stay, but I don't know that it'll work. He's set on doing this, and there is little to nothing that we can do to change his mind." She asked if ordering him not to die would work. "Yes. But do you want him here and happy while we can get him, or forever and heartbroken while he's here?"

"I don't want either thing to happen." The rest of the table agreed with her, but again, there was little for him to do to stop him from doing what he had his heart set on. "Sirous is a very good man, but he was also stubborn, and once set in his ways, there was no changing his mind. I know this as well as the rest of you do."

"Once I saw him chase a man for slighting him for years until he was able to find him. Then all he wanted was for him to say that he was sorry. I forget now what it was about, but he was determined to find him and make him do it. I almost felt sorry for the human. He had no idea what Sirous was talking about when he did catch up to him." The others had much the same sort of stories about their friend. His stubbornness was well-known, and they thought it was funny that anyone could change his mind once he'd made it up. "Not only did all he want from the man was an apology, but he and the human became good friends until his death some years later."

They each had stories like that of Sirous' stubbornness, and it was a good laugh for them all about him. He couldn't wait for him to come to the house with the others. Yosef was running late as he had things that he needed to pick up before coming to visit them all. He had a feeling that it was whatever blade he was planning to use on Sirous when the time came. Yosef might not want to do it, but he was true to his word when he made a promise to someone.

The rest of the evening was spent reaccounting times gone by. They talked about their childhood and how they'd always end up at his house when they were just starting out as vampires. This had been when his father had been alive, and it was nice to talk to people who had known him as well as he had. He had a lot of fond memories of his parents when they'd been together, and he was glad that his friends had some of the best memories of their life they'd told him while hanging out at his house all the time.

As they went up to their rooms one at a time, he stayed in the living room with his mom, and when Calla went up too, he told her how much he loved her, and she told him the same. As soon as she left, he asked his mom if she liked her or not.

"Of course I do. She's made you a better man for sure." He said that she made him want to be a better everything. "I can tell. It was the same with your father and me when we got together. You just find ways to make things better for the two of you all the time. She's very sweet, but I bet she can be a real ball buster when she's pushed into a corner."

"You've no idea. And I love that about her as well." His mom smiled at him, and he felt the warmth of her love all the way to his toes. "I don't want to sound ungrateful that you've come to visit, but other than meeting Calla, what did you come here for? I have a feeling that I'm not going to like it."

"You may well not. I've been thinking along the lines that Sirous has. It's been a lonely life without your father around, and I'm sick of it." He told her that he couldn't handle her leaving him. "I've been away for a long time, Brewster. We barely talked for the last century and a half. I know for a fact that you were thinking the same things as your friend."

"Yes, but I've since changed my mind. Stay with us now. We'd both love to have you staying with us for when the children come." She eyed him hard, and he smiled. "She's breeding now. We're to have a son in the early spring of next year."

"You wouldn't lie to me about that, would you?" He said he'd not do that to her. Especially in light of what she'd just told him. "Oh, Brewster, a child again. It's been so long that I'd given up hope of ever holding a grandchild of my own. Is she doing well? Taking good care of herself?"

"Yes. The doctor said she's doing very well and will have a good pregnancy so long as she eats more meat. He said that her weight is good and that she gets enough exercise. He's very happy with her." Mom looked so excited, he thought maybe she'd changed her mind about leaving him. "We're going to have more too. Not just the one centuries apart from any other kids we want to have. Calla Lily is excited and nervous, as you might well know."

"I can well imagine. I was the same with you when I found out that I was breeding. But your father, having all his brothers and sisters, was well acquainted with small ones running around. I have so regretted only having you as our only child." Mom clapped her hands and smiled at him. "You've given me hope, young man. Thank you for that. I needed that more than I even realized."

They talked for a bit more about the baby and other topics that would just pop into their heads. By the time he was headed up to bed after locking up the house, he was as happy as he was when he found out that Calla was breeding. They were going to be such a happy family that he couldn't wait to share the news with the rest of them. Tomorrow, tomorrow, he'd do just that.

Chapter 2

When the train stopped at the station, he didn't wait for the others to disembark but willed himself to the house of the king. He loved saying that. If anyone deserved to be king, it was his good friend Brew. He hoped for him a long life with lots of perks, as well as for his queen, the best life they could have. And he could see it too.

They would, of course, have their ups and downs, but for the most part, they'd have a wonderful life together with their children. He was happy for them to have so many, too, as he thought that six was the perfect number of children to have. Not that he had any of his own, but he could be happy for his best friend. Waiting at the door, he leapt back when, before he could ring the bell, a young woman opened the door and stared at him.

"You must be Calla." She nodded and asked him which one he was. "Sirous Smith. I believe that all the Smiths of the world are old shifters who can no longer lay claim to a last name if they ever had one."

"Brew said the same thing. Can I invite you in, or does it have to be Brew? He's not here right now, so it's either me or we sit out on the porch and wait for him while we get acquainted." He said that he honestly didn't know if she could invite him in, and she nodded. "Then you are welcome to our home, Sirous Smith."

He was not only able to step over the threshold, but he could feel the warmth of the home, too. It was as if the house was finally a home, and it wanted all that entered to feel its new status. He also had a feeling that it belonged solely to the woman in front of him and wouldn't be surprised if she was the only one who could invite people into the home. He'd have to ask about that when he got the chance.

"I'm not sure that I like you coming here if you're only going to die when we get to know you." Her bluntness startled him, and he felt his own monster curl around his body a bit for comfort. "You're making one of your dearest friends do the deed, isn't right? You should be ashamed of yourself."

"I'm not." She invited him into the living room, and he was delighted to see Mother Smith in the room as well. "It's been a long time. I had no idea that you'd be so beautiful after all this time. My goodness, you've not aged one bit."

"I'm with Calla in that I'm not sure you should be here when all you want to do is die. I will admit that this was my plan as well, but you've done this family wrong, Sirous, and I'm ashamed to call you one of my adoptive sons." He said that he didn't want it to be like this, that's why he didn't want it known what his plans were. "So you were going to just show up, get acquainted with all of us again, and then break our hearts when we felt your death? That's even worse than I thought, young man."

Few people could call him a young man and be right about it. He wished that Brew was here so that he'd have at least one person in the room who wasn't pissed off at him. Not that he believed that he'd be any less upset with him, but at least he'd not be so hostile about it. At least he hoped not. He wasn't entirely sure what to think about now.

He was given tea and wine when he had a seat. They were no less pissy with him, but at least they were trying to get to know him again. Especially Calla. She was the most beautiful creature he'd ever seen, and he was sure that Brew told her that daily. He knew he would have if he had a mate such as her.

When Brew came home, they hugged. He could feel the tension between Brew and Calla and had a feeling that he was the cause of it. Sirous didn't want to cause trouble when coming here and decided that if the others were going to be the same, he'd just leave. It wasn't like him to be a troublemaker, and he wasn't going to start that now so late in the game of his life. Whatever was left of it.

"I've been looking for someone to run a couple of businesses that I have around town. They're taking up too much of my time getting up and off the ground, so I thought having someone around to oversee them would be better." He asked what sort of businesses they were. "One of them uses old clothing to make braided rugs. I thought when I saw one of them that it was something from my past. Remember having one in our bedrooms when we were children? They were so warm and comforting that I didn't realize how much I missed them. The other is a shop that makes soaps and lotions and sells them. I wasn't sure how much business they could generate around here, but she swears she has an online presence that pays her bills. I know next to nothing about either place other than I loaned them the money to get started."

"You're still investing in the little businesses around here, aren't you?" He said that it wasn't him but Calla who saw something in them that she wanted to help them out. "Good for her. I don't think she likes me all that much."

Brew looked around and leaned in to talk to him. The women had gone to the kitchen when Calla said she wanted to get herself something to eat. Whatever they were doing, Brew didn't want his lovely mate to hear what he was saying to him about her.

"She is upset with you. I don't know that she

will ever not be if you go through with what you have planned. Yosef showed up yesterday and was telling us that he is to remove your head once you ask him to do it. He's also said that if you find your mate between now and then, he will not. I love that about him." Sirous asked him if he still loved him. "I do. Nothing you could do would change that. I will miss you and having you around, but I don't have to like you leaving us so soon after arriving."

"No, you don't, and I appreciate you not ordering me to not do this. This is something that I've given a great deal of thought about, and I'm ready. I have all my paperwork done so that the person I leave in charge will know just how to distribute my funds when I'm gone." He asked who it was. "It's you. I know of none better who will take care that my will is met with a strong heart and a good one. I have laid out the instructions well for you to follow."

They talked about his funds for a bit, and he was glad that he'd chosen Brew to do his final wishes. He wouldn't like the way things were in his death, not at all, but he'd do what he wanted and make sure that all his wishes were met with the rest of the men, too. Sirous had a great deal of money, lands, and gems that he'd collected over the centuries, and he wanted to make sure that they went to the right person when the time came.

When the front doorbell rang, he was excited to see that it was the other men. The three of them looked as good as they had forever, and he hugged them tightly. As soon as Calla and Mother Smith came back into the room, they included them in the conversations they were having, and it was a good time. He was going to miss this in the afterlife. If there was one. He didn't know, but he had hopes that there would be.

Sirous could still feel the cold shoulder he was getting from Calla. He hurt for that, knowing and seeing what sort of relationship she had with the others. He was sure that she'd not meant to be so cruel to him. Or perhaps she did. He didn't know her well enough to know how her mind was working on this. But he was hurt all the same.

They decided that they were going to walk around town to show what improvements had been made so far. Brew was quite proud of his little town, and it showed in not just the way he talked about it but in his mannerisms as well. Calla had had a great many ideas about what was happening around the town, too, and he was proud of her for voicing her concerns about details that he might not have thought about. Like she was concerned that if they did too much, people would begin to demand more things being done until there wasn't any money left. He could see that happening too. People with their hands out for every little project that needed to be taken care of.

"We're going to have council meetings here in the town. That way, some of the businesses can take advantage of new people being around and perhaps sell to them. Then there are the three bed and breakfasts that are here that could use the extra income from the other vampires that come around." He asked how often he was planning to have meetings that would involve other vampires. And would they be good while in town? "That was a concern of Calla's as well, and she came up with the law that if they were here on business, they couldn't feed on anyone who isn't willing. It will mean certain death for them should they break that law. I like it. It means we'll have peace here when there could be devastation if they get out of hand."

"That's going to work too. Right up until someone gets by with it. How are you going to monitor all the vamps that come around? I'm sure you have a plan." He laughed and looked at Calla. "You have a plan to make sure that vampires don't feed on others while they are here? You do know that it's second nature for us to feed when we need to."

"I'm going to keep an eye on them. I can tell where everyone is at any given moment when they're around. Say you were in the pack house talking to the head pack master. Not only would I know that you're there with him, but the conversation you'd be having with him. Not to mention all the others that might well be in the room with the two of you. It's a magic that I'm going to use to keep them in line. The first sign of someone taking what is not willfully given will be killed by removal of their head. I like how final that is."

She was talking about him, and he knew it. She was telling him that she would know when he was ready to die and that she'd be able to be there when it happened. He didn't know how that was going to work for her, but Sirous had a feeling that she'd use her considerable power and magic to make him suffer before he was dead, and there would be no one around to save him. He was toast if he crossed the young woman, and there would be nothing he could do about it himself, either.

The rest of the evening, they sat around and talked about times before. He mostly listened to what was being said and enjoyed some of the stories that were going around. At midnight, Calla left them to their talks and went up to bed. He could tell that Brew wanted to join her, but she had insisted that he stay with them as there wasn't going to be much time left for them to be all together again. Again, she was singling him out.

Sirous wanted to confront her, but there were two things stopping him. Brew was first and foremost in his mind. Brew would kill him and make him suffer if he so much as looked at his mate in the wrong way. He'd also make him suffer in ways that he had not thought of, too. Then the second thing was that she was his queen. Touching her or saying a cross word to her would bring down the council on his head, and while he'd be dead, he would suffer in ways that would make what Brew did to him seem like a walk in the park. They had been around forever and had perfected making vampires suffer at their hands. Or so he'd heard all his life.

They enjoyed their evening, and he was glad for that. While they'd been talking, Yosef had joined them, and they were all there now. The six of them had grown up together and had fought in so many wars together that they were more like brothers than friends. And he loved them more than he thought possible right now.

When he was shown his room, he was happy that he'd been told that he could enhance it in any way that he felt he needed. All he wanted was to have more room when he paced and to have lighting when he read. The bed was comfortable enough, but he changed it out for his own, knowing that he'd sleep better on it than the new one in the room. He also brought some of his paperwork with him to the new room so that he could finish up whatever he had going before next week.

He had a hard time remembering why he wanted to do this when he'd been around his friends and brothers. But as soon as he was alone, he felt the loneliness all over again, and it depressed him deeply. Next week, he'd be dead, and he found that he wasn't looking forward to it as much as he'd been before. But knowing as soon as this trip was over, he'd go back to wondering why he was still hanging around if he didn't do it. It was for the best that he went through with this now rather than put it off anymore.

~*~

Tabby knew that the wolves surrounding the property weren't wild ones. She knew that they were shifters and an old lot of them, too. But so long as they didn't bother her, she didn't bother with them either. They had allowed her to get a much-needed good night's sleep and had even shared their meat with her when they had it. Today, she was going to venture out of the woods and try to find herself someplace that would keep her safe from her mother. She was out to get her, and Tabby just wanted to be left alone.

"You're not supposed to be here." She knew the pack master for what he was and bowed before him. "You've been taught well, and I like that, but you're not supposed to be here. My men said you've been hiding out for the last several days now, and I'm only just now hearing about it."

"I meant them no harm, and it's not their fault that I'm here. I am hiding out and plan on finding myself other accommodations today when I make my way into town." He asked her who she was hiding from. "My mother. She has it in her head that I'd be better off dead than alive since she thinks that I have things and money that she could get off my dead body. I assure you that I have nothing more than the clothing on my back, and some of it was given to me yesterday by the pack you have here."

"They also told me that they'd been feeding you when you didn't have anything to eat. Is that true?" She asked him to not blame the men around the land, as she'd been the one begging for a meal. "So they said. I appreciate you being so honest with me, but for the third time, you're not supposed to be here."

"I promise you what I've said to you is true. I'm hiding from my mother." He said that he believed her, but why in the woods? "She's deathly afraid of the woods and what might be inside of them. The last time she tried to find me in some wooded area, she'd been nipped at by some animal, and now she swears that all woods are contaminated by wild beasts. I believe she still holds the marks of the animal now, and it has marred her looks. According to her, it's all my fault and just one more thing that she wants to kill me over."

"I have a feeling that it's more than that, but I'm

afraid that it will have to wait for another day. Today I'll take you to a house that sits on the property that we rent, and you can stay there. If she is so afraid of the forest and what's inside of it, she'll never find you unless you venture from it without my protection." She asked him why he'd go to so much trouble for her. "I was hiding away at one time from someone, and I know what it's like to have nothing but your fear to keep you company. If you'd like a job too, I have some things around the pack house that you could do as well. I pay a fair wage."

"I'll take it." He laughed, asking her if she wanted to know what it was. "Not if it pays a good wage. I'll do anything to be able to support myself while on the run. I've been beaten up so many times that I'm fearful that I'm all scars and nothing more."

"You're quite beautiful, as I'm sure you know." She shrugged, telling him in her own way that she didn't think that at all. "I'll take you there now, and we'll see about getting you some supplies. Like I said, so long as you stay in the wooded area around the building, you'll be fine. Beyond that, that's the best that I can do."

They talked about the building that she was going to be using as they walked across the creek bed where she'd been hiding. He told her that there was running water as well as a fireplace she could use to keep herself warm. He cautioned her about using it until they had a chance to have a look at it, and she agreed with him. There was no point in burning down the forest just because she wanted a warm bowl of soup rather than one straight out of the can.

It wasn't just a building but an old house. It had a good roof over it, and there was a wraparound porch that still had a couple of chairs on it. The windows were all dirty and green, but she didn't care so long as she could have a place of her own for a time. Even the bed, which looked new to her, was something that she was looking forward to resting on. She nearly hugged and kissed the big wolf, but didn't. She didn't want her scent on him so that others might find her. Her mother wasn't above having others look for her while she was hiding.

After being left alone to her own devices, she took a much-needed long, hot shower and used the equally new towels that had been laid out for her. The man must have worked very hard to have gotten the place ready for her, and she would forever be grateful to him for seeing to her needs instead of tossing her out of the first safe place she'd been in for years.

There was more to the story than her mother just wanting her dead and whatever she had on her. While they both knew that there wasn't any, it was the things that Tabby could do that her mother wanted her for.

She'd been born with the gift of sight, and her mother wanted to use it for her own needs, like the races and ball games that were being played. She'd be able to bet on them and come out the winner every time if she were given the correct answers as to who won those games. Not only was she able to see the games and who turned out to be the winner, but also other games of chance, too, like the lottery. Her mother didn't know about that just yet and was fearful that she'd find out sooner rather than later what she could do.

Making the little house her home, she was glad that Conri, the big wolf's name, had found her. More than likely, he could taste her magic on her; she'd been told by other powerful beings that it was easy to do, and had felt sorry for her. She didn't care, but she was going to do him a good job when she started working for him in the morning. Tabby didn't care what it was, the job, she'd do it with the best of her abilities and hope that he'd allow her to stay there forever. It was just the perfect place for her to lay low and take care of herself at the same time.

After the chimney was checked, she was able to start a small fire in the hearth. She had cans of food in the pantry that had been left for her, as well as a loaf of bread and some lunch meat in the working refrigerator. She was about as excited as she'd been in a while for some of the comforts of home at her fingertips.

After a much-needed shower, she was able to sit in the living area and read a book. It had been so long since she'd been able to do anything that was restful, and she was going to enjoy it. As she was getting ready for bed, she found some more clothing for her as well as some toiletries that she could use. Having a place to brush her teeth felt like heaven, and she was all the happier for it. Once she was in bed, it took her no time at all to fall asleep and not wake until the sun was coming up the next morning.

Stretching, she decided to take another shower just to wash the sleep out of her eyes. The water was hot and the spray was strong, so she was able to work out some of the tense muscles that her good night's sleep hadn't. Tabby was ready when the pack was at her door to take her to the pack house so she could get in a good day's work.

Hoping that the job was something she knew how to do, she was thankful for something to occupy her mind. It had been a long time since she'd been able to hold down any sort of job while looking over her shoulder all the time. Her mother had employed others to help find her, and they weren't as good at scoping her out as her mother could. It was almost as if she had a sixth sense about where she was all the time. Going into the packhouse, she was ready to begin her day. She was also happy that she'd remembered to bring her a sandwich for lunch so that she'd not have to leave the area and perhaps get caught. She wasn't going to jeopardize her new place to be safe for anything.

After a long day of filing things away for the big wolf, she headed home. She hadn't worked in so long that she thought she'd used up muscles that she'd not been able to use in a while. Especially her brain. Having a slight headache made her want to rest when she got home, and she laid down on the big bed. It was comforting to know that she could sleep without worries and wake up refreshed. She was going to like working for Conri, and she hoped that he would keep her around for a long time.

Taking a walk after her supper, she decided to see how far she could go before coming to the end of the woods. But before she got too much further than her home, she found a large man practicing with a sword. He seemed to know what he was doing with it, and she stood mesmerized for several minutes just watching him practice. He seemed to be determined or pissed off about having to practice, and she wondered why he was doing it at all. There were better things to work with than a sword. He could just use a log should he want to build up his upper body strength.

After watching him for another half hour, he left. She did as well, following the path to her home to get to bed early. She would have to work again in the morning and found herself looking forward to it. It made her day go by faster, and she liked that. But she did miss talking to someone at the end of her day. It was nice having a conversation just before bed.

By the fifth day, she had gotten everything filed that needed to be put away. Conri was happy with the way things were going and told her that she had the job, should she want it. He said that his desk had never been so cleared off, and he could actually sit down with his family at night and not have to worry about the mess he had in his office. She told him that she'd take the job so long as she could live in the house, and he said it was fine by him. It was good to have someone in the house, as squatters wouldn't be taking the thing over so long as she lived there.

"I have a group going into town tomorrow to get some supplies. If you make up a list of things that you need, I'll have them pick them up for you. By the way, there is a woman in town looking for you. I assumed it was your mother by the description that was given to me. She's asking a lot of questions." She asked if he was going to tell her where she was. "No, I'd never do that. You're here under my protection, and no one will say a word about you being here. Trust me when I tell you, she'll never get to you while I'm around."

"Why? Why are you protecting me like this? You don't know me. For all you know, I could be a mass murderer and have killed several people." He said there was something about her that made him need to protect her. Something about her said she was his sister. "You mean that I might be the mate to one of your brothers?"

"No. They've all been around here and know your scent now. You're not related to any of them. However, they feel the same way. This need to protect you. It might just be because you're a female down on her luck, but I don't know. There are a bunch of vampires nearby that I've come to love like my own brothers, so perhaps it's one of them. As I said, I don't know. But I will do what I need to make sure that you're safe." She told him about the man with the sword that she'd seen a couple of times now. "That would be one of the vampires. His name is Yosef. He's a good man. You should introduce yourself to him sometime. You'll like him. He has a duty to do soon, and he's not looking forward to it."

"What sort of duty?" He told her that he was to kill another vampire so that he could end his life. "He doesn't seem to want to do it as he's forever pissed off when he's out here practicing. I had no idea that he was going to kill someone. Is there any way that he can get out of it?"

"I don't think so. He made a promise, and he'll keep it no matter how it makes him feel about taking another life." She said that she felt sorry for him for making such a promise. "I do as well. Like I said, he's a good man and is only doing this because of a promise. And vampires hold onto promises like they do their mates. Very true to them both."

She decided that she was going to keep an eye out for the other vampire. She would tell him who she was and where she was staying. Perhaps when he did his duty to the other man, she would be far enough away that she'd not see it. The thought of beheading a man scared her, and she wanted nothing to do with it. Nor the two men involved.

Chapter 3

Sirous woke up bright and early the morning he was going to have his life ended. He had so many memories to take him to the afterlife that he hoped there would be someone there that he could share them with. If not, he could hold them next to his heart and be happy with the time that he'd had with them all.

He was especially sad to miss Calla. She never really warmed up to him, but she did tell him that her heart was going to be broken enough, and getting to know him was going to hurt her more. She had a wonderful heart, and he hated breaking it for her, but he knew that this was the way to go. He was going to end his life, and that would be better for all those around him. He looked at Yosef and asked him if he was still going to do it for him.

"I said that I would, and I won't break my promise this late in the game. I've about given up hope of you finding your mate, but there is still time. She might well be out there waiting for you and your demise to save you." He said that he hoped not. He would hate to leave her this early in their relationship. "I told you before. If you met her, I'm not going to end your life. You deserve happiness, and I shall laugh my ass off when she comes around the corner just as I'm about to do the deed. Mayhap she'll have a sister and we can bring in the day with a lot of sex and fun."

"It is only a few hours until we meet in the field. She would have to be right there when we're together before I could meet her. Nay, she's not going to find me in time. I know this as well as you do." He thought of having a mate at this late time in his life and shivered. "She would drive me to distraction, and we both know it. I'm too set in my ways for me to meet someone today. She would stake me in the heart, not that it would do her much good, but she might even remove my head for me, and then you'd be out of a job."

"I'd gladly give it to her, too." He asked him if he was all right. "Nay, I am not. To end your life is like ending a part of my own life. I do not want to do this, and I must have been very high on life when I agreed to do this for you. Either that or you tricked me. You have always been a trickster since we were small boys staying at the Smith's home."

"Aye, I was. It was a good time tricking you into doing things that you didn't wish to do. But we were just celebrating the mating of a good friend of ours when I made the pack with you. You said you'd do it if I hadn't found my mate in a thousand years. It's been nearly double that, and I'm still not looking for her." He asked him how long he had wished to die. "Long before the sun would no longer kill me. And it had been difficult not to greet the sun daily after that night. I've had a long life, as long as the others, but I know when I've had enough."

"I hate to see you go. Even if I wasn't doing the deed, I would hate to have you die. You've been a good friend all these years, and I'm sad that you have had such a horrible life that you wish to end it." He told him he'd had a good life, but it was too much anymore. "Too much? How can you say that when Brew has found his mate? I just know that she's out there and will save the day today. I have to believe that or what I'm doing hurts me too much."

They talked about anything but the impending death of himself. He remembered such good times with Yosef and wished at times there could be more. But just this morning, when he woke, he could feel the heavy weight of his life pulling him down. He'd seen many things in his life and had done just as many. Now it was time to put it all to rest.

At noon, Calla came to find him. She'd been asking him questions about his life since the second day that he'd met her. She still held him at a distance, and he didn't blame her. She had a tender heart, and what he was doing was going to break it for her. He only hoped that someday she'd forgive him and let him have peace with what he was planning.

At two in the afternoon, when all the others were resting, he and Yosef headed to the woods. He seemed to be looking for someone or something, and he ignored him for the most part. The woods were devoid of people this time of day, and that was the way that he wanted it. To have no witnesses to his demise.

"Are you ready?" His voice sounded loud in the afternoon sunlight. He asked him why he was yelling, and all he did was shrug. They'd found a stump that they could use for the beheading, and he knelt down in front of it. Just as he was ready to lay his head on the large wooden dais, he heard a noise that caused him to pause. "'Tis nothing but the wind. Go on. I'd like to get this over with before I change my mind again. This is not how I envision spending my final day with you."

He heard the noise again and turned to look for it. It was something like breaking twigs—his hearing being the best of the six of them, and he couldn't see anything. Laying his head on the stump, he closed his eyes. Telling Yosef that he was ready, he relaxed his body to the point of being ready to sleep when he felt something touch him from behind.

"Don't move." He said that he wouldn't and waited for the person to say something more. "You can't be serious about letting this man end your life."

"I am. If you'd like a front row seat, then go

ahead, but he's made a promise and I will hold him to
it." She said that no one was going to die today. "But
you see, he's made a promise and —" He turned to
look at her. "You've a gun. Not that it'll do you any
good to use on me. Had that worked, we wouldn't be
here like we are today. Go away with yourself. This is
what I want."

"Well, you're not going to be messing up
my woods with your blood all over the place." He
explained that he'd be ash when and if Yosef did it
right. He looked over at his friend, who was laughing.
"Go someplace else and do this then. There are plenty
of other places around here that can be used...what are
you doing now?"

He stood up. "This can't be happening to me."
He leaned into the beautiful woman and sniffed hard
at her throat. The temptation to taste her there was
too great, and he licked the pulse there until he was
pushed away. He looked at Yosef. "This is a trick of
yours, isn't it. Tell me that you've somehow made it
so that she smells like my mate, and I'll not be angry. I
promise that I won't."

"I did nothing but befriend a young woman
hiding out in the woods you picked. I told her that
we'd be here today and had her come and stop you.
As for her being your mate, I had no idea that would
happen, though I have to admit that it's the best news

that I've heard all my considerable life." He was still laughing, and he wanted to go over and use the sword on him. "Gives me hope that my own mate is out there someplace. This couldn't have come at a better time, admit it. She's your mate, and you can no longer go through with this deadly demand of yours."

"What makes you think she's my mate?" He said that he'd told him so. "No. I was mistaken. She's just a beautiful young woman who just so happens to be annoying me at the moment. Let's get on with this, and she can watch if she so wishes, but I demand my promise. I don't want a mate."

"Yet she stands before you. And she's having a rough time of it, too. Hiding out here in the pack woods from her mother. She's told me all about it. And what she's not told me, I've found out for myself. You have a mate, Sirous, and I, for one, would like to congratulate you on your find. May the two of you be as happy as you can be."

"I do not want a mate." He nearly stomped his foot, and that would have set Yosef off again. All the young woman was doing was staring at him, and he wanted to pull her into his arms and kiss her. Damn it all to fuck and back, this wasn't fair. He didn't want a mate. He had his own things to worry about, other than a young human mate that would more than likely irritate him for the rest of his days. "Why are you hiding in the woods? There have to be better accommodations than sleeping out in the open here."

"I'm hiding. You don't pay attention very well, do you? And what makes you think that I want a mate in you? I'm assuming that you're a vampire of considerable age. Is that the way you all dress in your time period? Who wears all black all the time? And you could get rid of that look on your face, too. I'm not any happier than you are about this shit." He didn't know whether to strangle her or feed from her. He'd not fed when he needed to, so that he'd be weaker when the time came for Yosef to kill him. Now all he could think about was feeding from the beautiful woman—

"What's your name?" She told him her name was Tabitha Williams, but everyone called her 'Tabby'. Then she asked who he was. "Sirous Smith. And I shant call you Tabby. Your name is beautiful, and I shall call you by your given name." He scrubbed his hand over his face and looked at her again. "We're in trouble here. I need to feed, and with that comes the idea that I want to fuck you too."

He was hoping to shock her, but she only pointed the gun at his head. He could almost wish that she'd pull the trigger; he was so confused as to what to do now. She was here. His mate after all these centuries, and he didn't have any idea what he was supposed to do about it. If he took her back to Brew's house, where he was staying, there would be no end to the teasing that he was going to get. And they'd be hard on him, too. All he'd wanted to do was to end his life, and now he had a mate for all time. Life sucked right now, and he was going to make sure that she knew that he had no use for one such as herself.

"I'll take care of you and make sure that you're safe, but I'm not going to fall in love with you." She said she didn't want anything from him. "Well, that's too bad. You're here now, and that's the way it goes. If you didn't want to find me, you should have stayed away. Now we're stuck with each other for all time, and there is nothing either of us can do about it."

"I can just leave you." She looked ready to bolt, and he put his hand on the gun she had. "Take it. Perhaps it would be a better way for you to go than to have someone remove your head." He explained to her about why he was having his head removed.

"So you see, now that Yosef isn't going to do the deed for me—after years and years of promises, you'll have to abide by my rules and live out your life with me." She turned on her heel and headed deeper into the woods. He was fine with that. He needed to think and couldn't do that with her standing around smelling like fresh flowers and sunshine. "Damn it all to fuck and back, I do not want a mate."

"Then turn her over to her mother." He looked

at his friend. "She'll gladly kill her off for you. Because the first time she asks her to use her magic for her and Tabby refuses, she's going to kill her. All you need to do is find the woman in town looking for her, and you won't have a mate anymore."

"I can't do that." Yosef shrugged and asked him why not. It wasn't as if he wanted her at all. "I don't want her, but I don't want her dead either. Where did she go just now?"

"She's living in a cabin not far from here. Conri set her up in it when he found her in the woods. She's been working for him, too, so that she can buy herself food when she wants it." He said that he'd take care of her needs. "Yet you don't want her. Make up your mind, friend, or she will. I don't think she's above finding a way to leave you now that you've found her, either. Since you never touched her, you don't have any contact with her. She's out there and could be hurt by someone, and you'd have no way of knowing."

"You're enjoying this entirely too much if you ask me." He said that he was actually. "Don't you feel the least bit sorry for me? I have a mate in my life, and I don't want one. What am I supposed to do with her now that she's found me? I have no idea what, as a mate, she'd even want from me."

"It's doubtful that she'd want a thing from you after the way you treated her." He said he was confused and angry. "And you took it out on her. She had no more idea that she was going to be your mate than I did. I had hoped. I like the young woman, but if you're going to continue to treat her like you have been, I'll gladly remove your head so that she doesn't have to suffer at your hand anymore."

"How can I be making her suffer? I only just found out what she is to me." He said that she'd left him instead of staying with him when he could be hurt by him. "You knew all along that you were never going to end my life. Admit it. You planted her in these woods so that I'd think she was my mate."

"Had I thought about it, I might well have, but my only plan was to let her stop you from killing yourself when there were witnesses. It worked out better than I could have planned." He was still laughing when he made his way back to the house. He'd be telling them, too, what had happened, and they'd all get a kick out of it. He was going to have to do something, or Calla would hate him worse than she did before. Sirous had no idea why it was so important that Calla not hate him. It was in the same manner that he didn't want Tabitha to hate him. Damn it, nothing was going the way that he wanted it to.

Looking for her was easy. Convincing her that he wasn't going to harm her was another thing altogether. She was in the house that she had hidden out in, and he couldn't get her to allow him in. Damn it, life was going to be harder just because he'd found his mate. And he didn't want one.

~*~

Tabby liked that the big vampire couldn't come into her house. That didn't stop him from yelling at the door for her to come and allow him in. But she could ignore that for now while she was thinking. There was no way that the vamp could be her mate. She didn't want a mate any more than he did, apparently, and now she was going to have to do what he told her. And there was nothing she could do about it.

She knew of a few mated couples. The one that she remembered most was the lion couple that lived down the street from her mother and her when she was a child. They fought all the time and made up just as frequently. If they weren't fighting, they were making love. Even at a young age, she knew that that was what they were doing. Her mother had had lovers in and out of their place all her life, and she knew that none of them were her uncles. It was her mother's way of getting back at her father when he'd left them. She didn't even know who he was, much less being able to pick him out of a lineup. The things that her mother had said about him made her think that she might well have been better off going with him. Mother was such a liar that she knew that if only a quarter of what she said about him was true, he was a saint compared to what she was. Then her mother had found out what she could do.

It was quite by accident that she let it slip that she knew the races. One of the men who had been staying with them had bet on the ponies, and she watched them on television with him. Every time he would place a bet, she'd make one in her head. For every time he was wrong, she was right, and she told the man so.

That was the first time that she got beaten by her mother when she gave him the winning horse names instead of her. The man, she couldn't remember his name, had been killed two weeks later when he tried to kidnap her from her mother. It was all over the papers about how he'd failed, and there was never any mention of how she could see the races. Her mom kept that little tidbit to herself.

Over the next ten years, she would be in and out of the hospital. She would only bet as much money as she had left over from some of the winnings. Her mother never knew how to save for a rainy day. It was a rainy day every day for her when he mother wanted more cash. After a while, she could see the lottery numbers too, but kept that to herself. By the time she was sixteen, not only had she moved out of the house with her mother, but she'd won enough money to keep her one step ahead of her when she was looking for her too. A couple of times, it was close, but she was able to keep out of her hands until the last year.

Her mother had hired someone to find her. It was a bear shifter that she'd given him some of her things so that he could track her. And so long as he didn't hurt her mind or face, he could do whatever he wanted to her when he found her. Christ, that was a nightmare just keeping herself alive long enough to get away again. He was big and mean and sort of stupid, too. When he'd cage her in something, he would take away her food and water, too; she'd be able to get away by using some of her magic that seemed to grow the older she got. It wasn't long before she could keep herself away from the bear when she needed to and out of harm's way. She'd been hiding on other people's property since then and knew that her mother wouldn't come and get her. The bear was just too stupid to look beyond the streets where she lived up until recently.

"I would like to have a conversation with you that doesn't have me screaming through the door at you." She'd forgotten about the vampire and was glad that she'd remembered that he couldn't get in unless she invited him. "Of course, that would be the only rule that you could remember about my kind. There are a lot of other ones that are out there, too, did you know that?"

"I don't know squat. And neither do you if you think I'm going to be all right with letting you in and around me. I like you not being able to come into my house." He cursed then. In several different languages, if she didn't miss her bet. "Such a potty mouth you have. You kiss your momma with that mouth?"

He called her childish. "Let me in and I promise not to hurt you. I also promise to take care of you and the situation with your mother. I know what sort of person she is, and she's lucky that I'm not going to be out to kill her anytime soon." She went to the door and opened it. "You only have to say that I'm welcome to enter, and that will allow me to come in and talk to you. I believe the wolves out here are having fun at my expense. They're laughing at me."

"Good for them. And I'd be laughing at you as well if I weren't so mad at you. What kind of person says he's going to feed from me and fuck me before we even know each other's names? Not anyone that I want to get to know, that's for sure." He said he'd forgotten he'd said that. "Well, I didn't. And you're not getting in here to do either of them. Just stay right where you are, and we can talk this way."

"All right. I'm sorry." She told him that wasn't good enough. "I'm sorry that I hurt your feelings. I know that I did, and that was uncalled for. But you have to see things my way. I never wanted to find you in the first place." She started to slam the door, and he stopped her. "That didn't come out right. I'm thousands of years old, and I've been a loner all my life. Finding you now, at what I considered the end, was startling and irritating. I've been trying to figure out a way to help you out of this predicament and not have to be mated to you at all. But there isn't any way, we're well and truly mates."

"I've been doing all right on my own, thank you very much. And the 'predicament' that you wish to get me out of is my mother. She wants the magic that I have." He asked her what it was. "I can see the winners of races and games. Not only that, but the lottery winnings, too. And don't ask me why I told you that last part, I have no idea. I just want to lead a normal life without someone right around the corner trying to kill me. She will, too, if I don't give her what she wants. She has the mentality that if she can have the winnings that I can get for her, then no one will. And I believe her when she says that."

"She sounds like a real peach. Is there anything else you can tell me about her? Like, does she have henchmen working for her?" Tabby told him about the bear shifter and the things that he's done to her when he found her. "I'll take care of him when I find him, too. At the very least, I'll get with his bruin leader. That will nip that in the bud. He'll more than likely kill him if I don't get to him first."

"Why would you kill him? He's done nothing wrong to you." She watched as he fought with what he wanted to say. And when he finally confessed to his reasons, she wasn't any happier with him than she'd been before. "Just because he hurts me doesn't mean that he needs you to kill him. Why does it seem like you're very killing happy? Do you generally go around killing people when they mess with your mate?"

"I've never had a mate before, so I have no idea. You and I will be learning what it is that I'll do to people who hurt you. My first instinct is to kill him, and I love the way that settles in my mind." She rolled her eyes at him. "This bear, do you know what color he is or where he started chasing you? I don't want to get the wrong one in trouble with his bruin."

"His name is Carl Wayne. He's a black bear from Ohio. The only reason I know that is because he told me one night after he locked me in the basement. If anyone deserves to be killed, it's my mother. She's done worse to me over the years. One time, she tried to sell me to the highest bidder online. And when that didn't work—she was actually surprised to find out that it's against the law to sell minors, or anyone for that matter, online. She knew, she just didn't care, so long as she was making money off of me." He again said she sounded like a peach. "Warm and fuzzy, she's not. More like the pit inside of it."

"I'll take care of her, too. And she'll not be bothering you again for money or anything else for that matter." She asked him if he was going to kill her. "If it comes to that. I'm not saying yes or no. Perhaps she has a quality about her that will make her redeemable." Tabby snorted, and Sirous smiled.

"If you believe that, then there isn't much redeemable about you either. She's not a nice person, and as far as I can tell, she never has been. Since I was an infant, she never cared for me." He asked her where he magic had come from. "I don't know. My dad was just a human, I was told, but the older I got, the stronger my magic was. At first, I didn't realize it was magic and thought it had to do with my brain, but once I was able to do other things, like hide in plain sight, I knew there was more to it than that. I've never had anyone tell me I was anything but human before."

"I could tell, but that would mean tasting you. And I know how you feel about me coming close to you." She asked him if he could really tell what she was by a simple taste of her blood. "I could tell if you have any shifters in your line and who they might be. As well as tell you if they were dead or alive as well. I'm old, an ancient that is way too old to be starting over with a mate in my life. But alas, here you are, and we're going to have to make it work."

"I don't really care if we do or not. As I said, I've gotten along well on my own. Not great, but well enough that I'm not dead yet." He told her that she was immortal. "When did that happen?"

"The moment that I realized that I belonged to you." He looked out over the fields where she was before looking at her again. "We'll have to go to the house now so that the others can meet you. I will warn you that they're an odd lot, but I love them."

"I'm sure they find something to love about you, too." He laughed, and she had to smile. "You don't do that often, do you? Laugh, I mean, you seem surprised when you do it."

"I've not had reason to laugh in a good long time, and it surprises me that you can bring it out of me so easily." She asked him how old he was. "Old. Thousands and thousands of years old, and I'm not even the oldest of our group. That would be Brew, and then there is his mother. She's a good woman. You'll get along well with her and Calla, Brew's mate."

"I'll go up to the house with you, but no funny business. No biting me or trying to get into my pants. I'll hurt you if you do try." He said that he'd refrain from trying anything with her until she asked him to do it. "Don't hold your breath on that, bucko. I'm stubborn too. In the event that you didn't get that."

As they walked up to the house, they talked

about what was going on with her mother and Carl. Carl wasn't a good person at all and would have raped her several times had she not gotten away from him. She thought that it would be good to keep that to herself. There is no telling what Sirous would do if he found that part out. He seemed like the jealous type to her. And she didn't need anything more to worry about.

Chapter 4

Linda didn't like waiting around. And no one in this stupid little town would tell her anything about her daughter. Perhaps she'd given them the winning horses at the races, but that would only get her into deeper trouble if she had. That money belonged to her. She'd just as soon kill her as to have her out doing nice things for other people. Linda had brought Tabby into this world, and she'd have no trouble whatsoever taking her out either. She should have let Carl do it. He'd make it messy and long.

"Are you Linda Williams?" She turned to look at the man and was upset that it was an officer. Telling him that's who she was had him nodding at her. "I've had several complaints about you harassing people about finding your daughter. You've been told no less than a dozen times that she's not been seen around here. Either settle that in your mind or leave. Those are your only two options."

"She's very dear to me, and I want her to be with me. A woman and her daughter need to be close, and Tabby has never been a dutiful daughter." He asked her why she'd want to be around someone who wasn't dutiful. "She's my only child, and I need her to be with me. She has some abilities that will make my golden years much better."

"You mean the races. You do know that there aren't any kind of races around here that you can have her betting on for you." She was shocked that he knew so much for not having been around her daughter and said as much to him. "I can read your mind, Ms. Williams, and it's not all that difficult. Wherever she is, I hope she's having a good time on her own. Now, I've told you what you must do to be welcome in this town, so either do that or move on. There isn't any way that anyone is going to help you find your daughter."

She knew that she was somewhere around here. Carl had been able to track her to this place, and she'd not moved on. There were plenty of places that she could hide out, but so far she'd not been able to find her at all. Linda wanted her daughter under lock and key and wouldn't rest until she was where she wanted her. There was too much at stake for her to just be running around telling other people how they could win the money that she thought belonged to her.

There had been a time when she had liked her daughter. It wasn't all that hard. She took care of her and kept the house cleaned up. There were times when food would suddenly appear in the cabinets, but she didn't worry over that. It wasn't until she found out that she knew the races that she really decided that she was worth more than a housekeeper.

Going back to the hotel that she'd been staying in, she went up to her room when the owner tried to get her to pay her bill. She didn't have the money right now, but would soon enough. As soon as she was able to get her daughter to cooperate, then she'd be in so much money that she wouldn't have to worry about it for a while. She would only admit this to herself. She was stupid when it came to money.

Linda would spend it as soon as it was in her hands. Even going so far as to spend what she didn't have. Like this hotel. Only the best would do, and she wanted the best for all time. There was no point in cutting corners when she had a daughter who would get her the world should she just come to heel. Damn it, but she hated her. To be given this gift and to squander it away like it was nothing was just plain mean. Not to mention selfish.

"How did I have such a selfish daughter?" She rarely spoke to herself but was willing to do so when there was no one around. As it was right now, the only people that were around her were cops and Carl. And he'd better be coming through soon, or she'd have to find someone else to find her. "I have ways of making his ass pay."

She knew his bruin leader well. Well, not well,

but she knew his name, and that would get his ass in trouble. She decided that she wasn't going to mess with him any longer and find a way to get him out of her hair. Even with the idea that he could have Tabby, the idiot couldn't catch her. She got away was all he ever said to her when she'd ask him about how much longer it was going to be before he was able to bring her to her.

Just as she was going to make a couple of calls on Carl's behalf, she looked out the window and saw Tabby walking along the street like she didn't have a care in the world. Rushing out the door, barely remembering to grab her key card, she was just ready to jerk her around to talk to her when she felt her arm being pulled up behind her back. The pain made her cross-eyed, and she was sick with it. She demanded to be let go.

"I don't think so. You touch what is mine, and you'll pay the consequences." She tried to tell the man who was holding her in such a painful way that she was her mother, but he didn't seem to care. "As I said, you touch what is mine, and I'll make you pay. You must be Linda Williams. I've heard a great deal about you over the last several hours. You're not a nice person, much less a good mother, are you?"

"I don't know what you're talking about. I was just happy to see my little girl when you pulled this shit on me. Let me go." He held her tighter while Tabby just stood there watching. "Aren't you going to do something? Tell him to let me go, and I won't hold this against you."

"You know, until just now I thought that I didn't care for Sirous, but you've changed my mind. He's good to have around." The man, she supposed his name was Sirous, thanked Tabby. "No problem. You can hold her all day for all I care. She's certainly done enough to me that was worse."

"The lies that come out of your mouth sometimes. I suppose you've told him about our little arrangement." She asked if she meant the ponies. "Yes." She looked around to see if anyone had heard her. That would be just like Tabby to blare out all her business to anyone around. "I demand that you help me out of this. And have him let me go. I have enough trouble walking around — where have you been hiding? I demand that you tell me right now."

"You demand a great deal for someone who is locked up with her arm behind her back. What is it that you want me to do? Tell you the winning races? I'm not going to do that. You'll just have to try and kill me. Which won't work anymore, I'm happy to say. I'm immortal." The man laughed, and she tried to look at him. "I'm sorry. I should have formally introduced you to the man who is going to marry me. Sirous

Smith, I'd like for you to meet my mother. And I only use that term because she did give birth to me, sadly. Mother, this is Sirous, my soon-to-be husband. And my protector, too. We are getting married, correct?"

"As soon as it can be arranged. What changed your mind?" She told him that she was going to be safer with him around. "That you will be. I promise on your heart that no one will harm you so long as I'm around. And I plan to be around for a good long time with you."

"Thank you." He said it was his pleasure, and Linda had had enough. Stomping her foot, she told the two of them to pay attention to her. "That's something else that I'd forgotten about, is how all the attention had to be on you when you were around. It's not always about you, you understand that, don't you? I mean, it could very well be about me. Like it is right now."

"Let me go." When she was freed, she nearly threw up; the pain took her breath away. "Christ, what did you do to me? I think you broke my shoulder. I'm going to sue you for everything you have. Then we'll see how much Tabby wants to stay with you. I'll bet before I win all your money, she'll be headed out the door."

"Not everyone is swayed by money alone. Perhaps she might love me one day. I already do her. Though I will admit that I wasn't so willing to fall in love with her at the beginning." Tabby told him that he was starting to grow on her, too. "Not like a fungus, I hope. I could be quite charming when I wish, and you make me want to be charming all the time."

"Of for the love of fuck, get a room. But not before Tabby gives me the winning races for today. I have bills to catch up on and people to pay off." Again, Tabby told her no, she wasn't going to do that anymore. "You will when I finish with you." The big man growled, and she thought that was funny. "What are you anyway? You have to be something other than human. No one would want my daughter without some sort of incentive going on. Is it the races? What did she tell you about them? That's my money if she's already told you the winners for today."

"Vampire." There wasn't too much that she was afraid of other than the wooded areas, and that was a vampire. They could kill you easily enough without having to be in the same room with you. Not to mention draining you dry before you knew he was sucking on your neck. Shivering, she took a step back from him and watched him carefully. "I see you've gained some smarts over the years. I will kill you, Linda Williams, if you don't leave my lovely bride alone. I'm not above draining you dry, either, though I think that the blood would surely be tainted. I'm warning you for the last time to leave my Tabitha alone, or I shall show no more mercy on you than you did your child."

"I'm not afraid of you." But she was, and she had a feeling that he knew it to be true, too. "You're just another notch in my bedpost on things that I've taken out when they get too close to what is mine. And she is mine, too, don't you ever forget it."

"I have no fear of your threats. Because that's all they are, but threats. However, if you harm even a hair on her head, I will kill you in ways that you won't ever understand. You'll suffer too, and by that I mean for months before I allow you to die." Linda felt her blood run cold at his promise. For there was no doubt that what he was saying to her was a promise. He would do just as he said he would and make her death something that she'd beg for, and still, he'd show her no mercy. "Have we come to an understanding, you and I?"

"I understand that you're going to pay for this. I'm going to sue you, and I'm going to get my child to do what I tell her to do. She knows better. I have people in places to make her regret even being born." Tabby said that she already regretted being born to her. "What an ungrateful cur you've turned out to be. After all that I've done for you, you have the nerve to treat me like this. You're going to pay, Tabby. I promise you that you're going to pay. Now give me the races before I have to hurt you while you stand there."

"As I have said to you several times now, no.

And I'm no longer afraid of you." She turned her back on her, and Linda saw red. She would have hit her, too, had she not been still sick with pain. Whatever he'd done to her, it wasn't getting any better with him no longer holding her. "I'm going to this Brew's house and get to meet a bunch of other vampires that might well be nicer to me than you've ever been."

"I'll escort you. I think that we've said all that can be said on the matter of keeping Tabatha safe." Sirous looked at her, and she could feel him in her mind. At his laughter, she took two more steps back. It wasn't full of humor at all, but a scary sound that made the hair on the back of her neck stand up.

"If you cross me even one time, there will not be a second time. Do I make myself clear to you?"

"I know what you are now. What do you think this town will say when they have a nest of vampires around killing off their children?" She didn't feel him move, but suddenly she was choking and several inches from the sidewalk. Grabbing at nothing around her throat, she stared at the man in front of her with fear. He was going to kill her, and there was nothing that she could do about it.

"This is only a taste of what I'll do to you." He moved then, snapping his fingers so that she was released and dropped to the ground. "I have your scent and your taste now. I will know your every thought so long as you live. Which won't be all that much longer, the way things are going with you."

Then he was gone. Just like a poof of air, he was not only gone, but she couldn't see Tabby either. Staying on the sidewalk, she tried to tell herself that it hadn't been as bad as she had thought it was. He'd made her feel like he was going to kill her, and she wasn't near death. However, every time she touched her fingers to her throat, she could feel the pain there. That was when she noticed the blood. Christ, he really had bitten her, and now she was going to be his slave forever.

~*~

Sirous had never been so angry in his life. And it felt good. He'd not only made his point to the other woman, but he knew things about her that he doubted that she knew about herself. She was dying of cancer, and it would be less than a year before she would succumb to the disease. He should just let her suffer that way; it was hard on a human, he knew this. As he caught up with Tabby, she took his hand into hers. The feeling of anger not only dissipated, but it seemed to just evaporate like it had never been an issue. He kissed the back of her hand before they rang the bell to Brew's home.

"I was wrong about your mother being a peach. I believe that she's every sour fruit I've ever seen."

That brought a burst of laughter from her as well as tears. "Don't cry, my love. I didn't kill her. Though I will admit if anyone deserves it, she would be the one. I've never met a more vile woman in all my lifetimes."

"Will you protect me from her and all the people she has on her payroll? Though I don't know how she has any money to pay them, she's never been one to do anything correctly." He said that he'd go to the ends of the earth to protect her from everyone who dared harm her. "Carl Wayne? He's going to be a problem. I've seen him around town."

"I've gotten in contact with his leader. He's none too happy with the things I was able to enlighten him about. I doubt very much by this time tomorrow Carl will be around to bother anyone. I made it perfectly clear that to harm you is certain death to all who are involved. And by me telling him, that made him as involved as Carl is. Nay, he'll never harm you again, or a burin will cease to exist." He thought about some of the things that Tabitha had said to her mother. "Am I really growing on you? I should think that I'm not such a bad man now that you've made it clear that I'm not to touch you unless you wish it."

"I honestly don't know what it is that I want." She rang the doorbell. "I only hope that the rest of the people behind this door are as nice as you can be when it suits you."

The door was opened before he could come up with a good reply. She'd been catching him off guard since he'd met her, and he was sure that for the rest of their lives together, she would still do the same. Instead of being upset by her candor, he was enjoying it. He wasn't sure what was wrong with him, other than he really was falling in love with his beautiful mate.

The others were welcoming to her when the two of them entered the living room. He knew that Yosef had told them all the story of how they had met, so he saw no reason to go over it again. However, Brew thought it was just funny enough to bear repeating, and he wanted to strangle the man when he brought up his first words to Tabitha. How he'd been tricked into having a mate at the point where he wanted to end his life. Calla sat down next to his dear heart and was talking to her when he was hugged by Brew.

"I knew she was out there for you. I just knew it. And now that you'll not be ending your life—you aren't, are you?" He said that he wasn't, as he had found someone to keep him safe. "I should hope so. And I welcome her to my house. I know she's been hiding from her mother, Yosef told us all about it. She'll not have any troubles around here anymore. I swear to you on my mother's heart there will be no one to harm her again."

"I've taken care that the bear has been taken

care of as well." Brew told him that was the next thing he was going to ask him about. "I don't believe he'll be around much longer if he's not already dead. I made it perfectly clear that I will bring harm down on the entirety of the bruin should he be left to continue what he's been up to."

He told him about the incident involving Tabitha's mother. He also shared with him that the woman didn't have much longer to live, even if he were to leave her alone. Sirous knew that he'd not be leaving the woman alone. She was going to continue to cause trouble from now on, and she'd be in his sights just when she started to cause trouble again. He wasn't above having her arrested, either, just so that she'd be out of their lives for a bit.

"She has it in her head that Tabitha will cave if she were to do something to me. Her plan is to tell the town that you have a nest going on here and that we spell certain death to all the children. Why is it that you suppose that that's the one thing that people believe about us? That we feed on children? I've never once had a meal on a child, and I doubt very much any of the rest of us have either." Brew said that not even when he'd been desperate had he ever done such a thing. "There you go. Someone said it once, and instead of finding out if it was true or not, they believed it. Humans are so gullible."

"I like this new you. You've barely said ten things strung together, and now here you are having a full conversation with me. I really have missed the old you." He said that he'd not had a reason to be talkative before. "A mate can really change your mind about things, can't they? This morning, you thought that this was the last day of your life, and it turns out it was the first day of your life with a mate. How does she like being mated to a vampire? Has she busted your chops about it?"

"She's very good at busting my chops, as you put it, about everything. She has rules about me taking her and feeding from her. Until we arrived here, I've not even touched her, but for my wishful thinking. She's a beauty, is she not?" He said that she was very beautiful. "I find that I could stare at her all the time and see something different each time I look at her." He looked at Brew. "You tell anyone I said that and I'll wring your neck. I don't know what's wrong with me all of a sudden."

"You have a mate that's all." He asked him about living arrangements. "Not that you're not welcome here for as long as the two of you wish, but I'm sure that now that you have her in your life, you'll wish for your own home."

"I don't know. We've only just met today. I will be looking for something for us. With her, no doubt, but as for any other arrangements, I think we'll have to wait on her. She has a willful mind, and I'd hate to upset her by assuming that she's going to want a home of her own. However, she did like the house that Conri gave her. You should see it. It's as clean as a whistle and flowers all over the room that I could see into." He asked if he was able to go into the house to stay with her. "She wouldn't allow me to go into her home. She's smart in that. I don't know what I would have done had she allowed me to enter. I know that I wasn't in the best frame of mind when she was in there without me."

"You two will get to know one another in no time." Sirous hoped so. He really was falling in love with the pretty little human. "I take it that you've not figured out how she knows what she does about the winners. I could tell her if she didn't trust you."

"I don't know that I could take that either, my dear friend." There was only a bit of jealousy when Brew suggested he bite his mate before he did. He was sure that he understood, too. Brew was a good man and a better vampire than he had been.

For the rest of the evening, they spoke of nothing to do with Tabitha's mother or the bear Carl. It was a time of good friends, and he thought that perhaps he had the best of the lot. When Mother Smith joined them, she brought up stories of their childhood and how they'd all grown up together under her roof.

As children, they had spent a great deal of time in the Smith household. She'd only been known as mother and her mate as father, even though they all had parents of their own. Sirous' parents had been distant when he'd been a child. So much so that when he felt their deaths, it was nothing more than a feeling of relief. The same had been with Kenneth's parents, too. They'd been old when they'd had them, and they, like him, had been set in their ways too much to want to bother with them. Mother Smith had made up for their lack of love and encouragement by making sure that they had a bed at their home and all the knowledge they'd need to become good men. He knew, too, how to woo a woman; however, he'd not had much of a reason to use it until now. He was going to make sure that he dusted off that knowledge and used it to woo his mate. She deserved the very best.

By the time the younger women were yawning their way through conversations, he knew it was time that he made a decision on where they were going to be staying. He wouldn't presume to sleep with her, but he would find her a good bed that she could rest in with him nearby. Calla had made the arrangements for him, and he would be forever grateful to her for taking it upon herself to make sure that Tabitha felt welcome in the big home.

After the women went up to bed, he longed for a night out with his friends. He'd been pushing them away because he knew that to get too close to them again would be harder on him, but now that that part of his life was at a close, he wanted to spend as much time with them as he could. They all decided that they would walk into town and see what they could get into. Brew and he wouldn't participate in the feeding, but they'd have fun all the same. He'd forgotten what it was like to spend the evening with a bunch of vampires on the hunt for a meal.

By the time the sun was coming up, he was beginning to feel the pull of his rest. He didn't have to rest as much as a newborn vampire did, but he'd been neglecting his rest for trying to get in as much time with his friends as he could. Now all he wanted to do was to sleep the sleep of his kind and not wake until he was better. He would have to feed soon, and he wasn't going to mess up with Tabitha by smelling of someone else when he had her to be his mate.

Checking on Tabitha before he had his slumber, he knew that she was sleeping well and left her to it. As much as he wanted to just rest next to her, he knew that all the trust that he'd built up until now would be gone if he were to do that. Instead, he made his way to the room he'd been using and laid down. Sleep took him in its grip even as he thought about making sure that the house was well protected for the only true one of his life. His mate deserved the very best, and he was going to make sure that she had it.

When he woke the next evening, he felt like he'd gotten a good day's sleep. Nothing had bothered him, and he found that Tabitha had gotten up long before he did. Going to the kitchen, a place that seemed to call to the others too to spend time, he found her having a hearty breakfast and talking with the faeries of the house. He'd forgotten they were around and was glad that someone had introduced her to them. Calla was warmer towards not just him but Tabitha, too.

"I knew that something would happen and you'd not have to go through with your death." He said that he was humbled in the way that he'd met her. "As you should be. She was just telling me how you were going to protect her from her mother. I hope you know that if you were to kill her, I'd not lose any sleep over it. She sounds like a monster."

"That's a good name for her, monster. I do believe that she's that and more." Calla told him that she would kill her herself if given the opportunity. "For now, I'm going to allow her to live. But as soon as she tries anything with my heart, I'm going to kill her just the way that I warned her. Slow and painfully."

For the rest of the evening, they talked about the upcoming festival that was coming to town. Calla wasn't all that thrilled about the rides, as she'd heard all her life that they weren't well-maintained and were dangerous to be ridden. He assured her that he'd take care that they were safe while in town to keep the children safe. He found that he really was a different man than he'd been even one day ago. Before, he wouldn't have cared at all for the rides and the children on them. Now he wanted nothing to happen to anyone who came around him. Sirous not only made the rides safer, but he also made sure that there was no cheating going on with the games along the way, too. It was the least he could do for his new hometown.

"We need to talk." He told Tabitha that he was there for her. "I've heard a great deal about vampires and more last night. I don't know what to believe." He told her that she only needed to ask and he'd tell her. "I don't know about you either. You're so different than you were when I first met you. It's like you're a pod person."

While he didn't know what that meant, he did strive to answer all her questions about his kind. Before the end of the evening, he was sure that he'd given her every answer that he could have about vampires and what they did than he'd ever thought about in his life. He was happy too. Happy that she was willing enough to question him about his kind so that she'd not be fearful of him. That made him happiest of all.

Chapter 5

It took her most of the morning to get through to Conri. She wanted to tell him that she was no longer living in the house that he'd provided for her and to thank him for his generosity. She doubted that most would have seen how down on their luck she'd been and taken her in. She was glad that he'd done what he'd done and made her feel welcome, too. She liked the older wolf and was also glad that he sent the wolves with her when she'd been walking along the path to his place.

"Tabby, my dear, it's so good to see you." He hugged her, then pulled away. "I'd not realized that you'd found your mate. Good for you and him. Who is it? Rutger? I'm betting that it's Yosef. I heard that he'd been hanging around the woods."

"It's Sirous. You know him?" He said that he did indeed know the old vamp and was glad that she'd brought him out of his shell. "I don't know about all that, but he is different from what he had been before. He's nicer anyway."

"As he would be. Getting a new outlook on life can do that to a man. So is the house...I would suppose that you no longer have a need for the home that you've been staying in. You must be looking for something bigger." She told him she was staying at Brew and Calla's home for now. "I would imagine that you'll be moving out on your own soon. Good luck to you. This town has some nice homes in it if you only know where to look."

"I wouldn't know anything about the housing market around here. I don't believe that Sirous and I have gotten that far in our relationship yet, anyway. We're still getting to know one another." He nodded as if he understood. "I came here to thank you for what you've done for me. The house was just what I needed to keep me safe for a while. I appreciate it too if you were to thank the other wolves that walked me around, too, as I'm grateful for all their help as well. I don't think I would have been as safe without them around all the time."

"I heard about the bear that's been chasing you. I also heard that his bruin has taken care of him. I can give you details on that should you want them, but I'd rather not. Suffice it to say he's been dealt with in a way that won't have him bothering you again." She'd heard that too and was glad that she didn't have to worry about the man or beast anymore. "I would like to tell you too that so long as you're on the property of Brew's home, you will be protected. We roam the property so that nothing gets into the land where his mate is. You are just as precious to us as she is."

"Thank you." She was invited to have a seat but declined. "I must get back to the house. I left without telling anyone where I was going. Though I think Rutger did. He was the only one up when I left the house."

He cautioned her about that, and she agreed. "They won't know that you're missing if you don't tell someone where you've gone. At the very least, let the cook know where you've gone so that in the event you're taken, though I don't know how that would happen, you will be missed when you don't show up to where you're going."

"I'll do that from now on. I'm not used to people caring where I am at any given moment. I guess that's one more thing that I'm going to have to get used to." She wanted to cry. Or at least have someone talk to her about vampires and her mother. She was already sick of rules, and there hadn't been that many of them as yet. Getting to the door seemed to be imperative, so she made her way there now before she became sobby. While most of her life was good now, she was more lonely than she'd ever been in her life. And all because she'd met her mate one afternoon and things had changed.

"What's the matter, dearie? You look ready to burst into tears. I've not done anything to you, have I?

I'm profoundly sorry if I've misspoken to you about something." She did cry then, and her sobs brought her closer to Conri when he pulled her into his arms. "Please tell me what's wrong before a big vamp comes to destroy me for making you cry."

"I'm lonely and I have no one to talk to but about things that I'm doing wrong." She cried all the harder and felt stupid for it. "I know you don't know me all that well, but you've been so kind to me since I met you. Everyone at the house is either a vampire or about to be one. I have nothing in common with them." She heard the pounding at the door and looked in that direction.

"I'm sorry, love, but Sirous is at my door now. Make sure you tell him all that before he murders me. I can't be killed any more than he can, but I know, too, that he can put me in a world of hurt." She said she was sorry. "I'm not. It's not often that I get to be the hero to someone else's mate. Come on, we'll meet him there together so that he can see that I've not harmed you in any way. He'll be there for you should you tell him what you told me. I promise you that he only wants the best for you."

He was at the door, at least she thought it was him. His eyes had turned, and he looked like the monster that she'd heard he could be. As soon as she went into his arms, he changed again into the man that she'd come to know. Looking up at him, she asked if he really would have killed Conri.

"Nay. I would have asked first. I think I would have. He's a good man and has been telling me what has you so upset. I can understand that. We've spoken of nothing else but what it means for you to be living with a vampire. Tomorrow we shall go and find ourselves a house that we can live in near Brew. Nothing will be said about anything that you don't approve of, either."

"Don't patronize me." He said that he'd never do that, but understood about being lonely. He was sick of talking about the past, too, and all the talk about vampires. "There are more to the world than just your kind. Also, I'm ready for you to taste me. I don't know how much you need from me to feed, but that's all right too. You've done so much for me that I feel sort of selfish about keeping you from being healthy."

"I'm healthy. And for as old as I am, it doesn't take all that much to feed me anymore." He grinned at her then. "However, I will tell you this one thing about vampires. Your blood will be all the richer if you'll allow me to make you come when I drink from you. That is true."

"I wondered about that." They walked hand in hand back to Brew's home. She saw her mother once, but she didn't see her. Brew had told her before she'd had her breakfast that she was going to be arrested soon for not paying her bill at the hotel. She'd accumulated a large bill in the two weeks she'd been there. "She was counting on me to pay for it for her. It's always about money with her."

"She's not unlike some humans and will forever take the easy way out of something if they can. Not all, but a lot of them will do that." She said that her mother had been doing that since she was a child. "No more talk about your mother, either. We'll deem this day to be all about having some fun. I think that I can remember how to have fun again."

She didn't know how he'd done it, but he had a list of places that they could look into buying. Tabby did ask him how much he could afford, and he told her about the money that was coming to her from the burin. The leader had insisted that she get whatever had been Carl's for whatever pain and suffering he'd caused her. She was almost all right with that, but thinking that he'd had to die for her to get it put a damper on it. But Sirous assured her that he had more than enough money to buy any home they wished, and he'd be able to furnish it as well.

"I have more than enough money in investments that neither of us would ever have to work again throughout our lives and still have more than enough left over to purchase whatever we want from now on." He told her that he'd been investing since he was a young vampire. "So you see, there is no reason for you to ever use your special magic again should you wish not to."

True to his word, they spoke of nothing but things about the house and money. It never got boring; however, she was happy to know that he was never going to require her to use whatever she had unless she wanted to. And in her heart, she knew that it wasn't anything that she wished she had to use. Not even for her mother, though she had no doubt that she'd be demanding again when she got out of jail.

They found two houses that they liked. One of them was a huge antebellum sort of house that they both fell in love with. It would need some work to get it up to this century, but he told her that with the help of the faeries, they'd be living in it as soon as the loan was approved. That worried her a bit as he said that he had money, but he assured her that it was good for the town to borrow money from the bank instead of paying cash for the house. She hoped he was right. She didn't want to have to use the magic now that he'd told her that she'd not have to.

They put a bid on both houses, with him telling her that he could use the other house as a rental for the extra income. She was fine with that and told him so. As soon as they were finished with the paperwork, both homes had been approved for their purchase, and she had to choose which one she wanted. It wasn't a hard decision; she picked the first house they'd seen, of course. Now all they needed was furniture, and they'd be able to move in. Sort of.

"I was wondering if we could get a cleaning crew to go in and clean it from top to bottom? That way we're not cleaning while the furniture is waiting to be brought in." He thought that was an excellent idea and told her that he'd get the faeries right on it. They loved to clean. "They're so tiny. How much work can they do?"

"They might be tiny, but there are a great many of them. Brew was telling me that they keep their home clean without much thought. Even going so far as to run the vacuum cleaner once a day. I'd like to see that sometime, but I fear that I'd hurt myself laughing so hard." She tried to think about how a tiny little person would be able to do that, too, and grinned. "Now I see you get the image. I wondered too if they wear maids' outfits when they work. Now that I think I'd pay good money to see."

They talked about the faeries, and she was startled when one of them came to sit upon her knee. They'd stopped for some lunch and were sitting at a picnic table near the Dairy Mart. When he bowed to her, she nodded her head at him.

"My name is Soot. I didn't know what it was

when I chose that name, so I'm stuck with it." She smiled at him when he grinned. He had very sharp teeth and a sword at his back. "I will be with you forever, my lady. I will be there for you when you should need anything at all."

"I don't know that I need anything right now. Except for our new house to be cleaned up. But that would take you forever." He assured her that there were many more who would love to work with her. "I need to know how to pay you. We've talked about it, Sirous and I, but we don't know what to pay you with. I'm sure that our money wouldn't mean that much to you. Not to mention how you would carry it around." A short giggle burst from her mouth. "I'm sorry. We've been having fun today."

"As well you should. Both you and Lord Sirous should be having lots of fun now that you've found one another." He bowed to her again, and she put out her finger to shake his hand. When he did so, she felt a bit of something wash over her. "We have a connection now, the two of us. Whenever you need me, you need only to say my name and I'll be there in no time. As for the house, it would be our pleasure to do this for someone as kind as you are."

"Thank you." He flittered a bit then asked her for permission to leave. When she granted it, he simply disappeared. She thought that trick would be nice when she didn't want to talk to someone, like her mother. Sirous introduced her to his faerie named Lana. She too was going to work on the house to be cleaned up, and she was sure by the end of the day they'd have move-in-ready homes. At least she hoped so.

~*~

Sirous had never enjoyed shopping before. But today he thought that he could spend the entire day doing just that. He was sure it had a lot to do with Tabitha, but he didn't care what it was; he was getting to spend time with her, and they were laughing a great deal. He looked at the couch they'd been debating on buying. It was a comfy couch, but it wasn't in the color they wanted.

"You think that the faeries could change the color once we get it home?" He said he'd not thought of that but was sure that he could do it as well. "Then we'll get it. I hate the color. I thought all places that sold furniture had choices that you could pick from for the material. Not only is this thing ugly, but the material is scratchy as well."

"I believe I had one like this in the seventies. It was all the rage to have one of the most uncomfortable couches around. I don't believe anyone ever sat on it. Not so long as I was in the house, I don't think." She laughed, and he thought he could make it so she laughed all the time. He certainly enjoyed it. "I do hope that the fad isn't returning. It will make for a lot of uncomfortable guests when they come over."

"Do you entertain much?" He told her that he'd had no reason to entertain until she came along. "I've never had company come over for any reason. I went to work and came home afterwards. It was not only lonely, but it was also cheaper to be alone all the time. I never really struggled for money, but if there had been an emergency, I would have been screwed."

He told her about his life as a man growing up when things were so different from what they were right now. There were no cars at all, and only the rich could afford a horse. "Unless they were farmers, and they had one long before anyone else did. I worked on a farm once. It was something that I decided I wasn't cut out for. All that rising before the sun came out was hard on me."

"I bet it was." She smiled at him. "You're very easy to talk to, did you know that? You're very sweet too when you want to be." He told her that she brought out the best in him. "I'm glad to hear that. You do the same for me. I feel like a new person when you're around me."

"You make me want to be a better person than I have been. I was set in my ways and never thought that a mate would be able to stand me. I'm glad that I'm wearing you down." She laughed, and he had to smile. It sounded so natural for her to laugh at him. And he found that he didn't care one bit that she was. It was as if he really had become a different person. "Well, we have work to do. I think we've decided on this couch and the love seat that goes with it. However, I think we should order two of the same so that there is enough room in the living room for people to sit. We're all big men, and I'd hate to crowd them onto one couch when they come to visit us."

They talked about anything they wanted. She would occasionally ask him a question about his life or that of a vampire, and he'd tell her. He didn't get into the gory details of his life; he thought that would give her nightmares for the rest of her life. By the time they were ready to go home again, not only had they filled out most of the house, but they'd been able to pick up things for the walls as well.

"I have several houses that I go to when I need a break. I've never thought of them being in a good location for a mate. But one of them is in France. I have houses all over the world, as a matter of fact. We should go to them and enjoy ourselves. I know that there is staff at each of them, but I'm almost too worried about what the houses might look like now that I think about it." He told her how Calla had found that Brew was paying a dead woman who had worked for him many years ago and thought about asking her to go over his books. "I do my own, but I'm sure that I'm missing something important when I just glance at them at the end of the month."

"I used to be an accountant. Well, I suppose that I still am. I could do that for you. Unless you'd rather have Calla do it. She seems to enjoy it a great deal." He thought it would go a long way in showing her that they had plenty of money if she were to do them for the household. He told her that he'd be happy with her doing them. "I'll start on them as soon as we're settled. I might even find a thing or two that you've done wrong. You seem so perfect to me right now."

"Thank you. You're making me blush." When she smiled at him, he could have taken on the biggest monster in the world and come out on top. He nearly pointed out that he'd only blushed once before in his life, and that was a story that was better left untold.

He'd been a mere child when he'd seen his first naked woman. Upon reflection, she'd been neither young nor good-looking, but she'd been his first, and that had been an experience that he never forgot. Nor would she him had she still been alive.

But he did tell her of stories that he thought she might get a kick out of, like his first car ride and his first time on a horse. Neither had turned out right for him, and he'd nearly been killed when the car he'd been driving hadn't had any brakes. Most of the day had been spent in good conversation like that. She also told him of her life, and he felt sorry for her as she'd not had a good life, not even as a child.

"There was never a time when we celebrated the holidays. I remember one Thanksgiving that we were dressed to go someplace to eat, and mother had gambled away all our money. She knew about my abilities by then, but since it was a holiday, there were no races that I could give her. That got me a night locked in the closet with the light off and no supper. She would blame me for her inadequacies all the time. After a while, you get used to that sort of treatment, I guess." She smiled at him. "Tell me something more about your life so that I'm not feeling down again. She does that to me every time I talk about her."

"Before I forget to tell you, the money is there for you from the burin. It's a considerable sum too. I guess this Wayne person knew how to invest his money from your mother, and he did well with the ponies as well when she did. I never bet on something that is supposed to be a sure thing, but I guess people do win those sorts of things."

"How did you get your money? I mean, did you start out life as a vampire with funds?" He said that he'd been from a very wealthy family, much like the others in their group. "So when they died, you inherited it all. I guess that's a good way to have funds.

I never knew who my other family was. For all I know, they could have been wealthy as well."

"Your mother would have had to have gotten her money from somewhere, knowing how she gambles. I would imagine that they cut her off when she'd been growing up, or they might well have been as broke as she was when she was arrested." He'd told her again about her mother being taken to jail, and she had a couple of questions about that, too. "She went without too much in the way of fanfare. I guess she told them that you were going to pay her bail, and there hadn't been one set as yet. Being such a small town, about those kinds of things, we'll have to wait until the circuit judge comes through or take her to Zanesville for a hearing there. She's racked up quite a bill at the hotel, and she made a mess of the room as well."

"That sounds like something she'd do. Make a mess of something that didn't belong to her. She never kept house either. That was something that fell to me as well." He took her into his arms and held her while she looked so sad. "How can a person who is supposed to love you treat you so terribly? I was only a kid that she took advantage of all the time. Then, when she found out what I could do, it was like I was only good for one thing."

"I'm sure to her you were." He realized that he shouldn't have said that, but it was out now, and he held her when she started to cry. Pulling the shadows around them so they'd have some privacy, he let her cry out all her misery while he held her tightly in his arms. "I love you, Tabitha. You're the best thing that has ever happened to me. And I would shout it to the world, given the chance."

"Thank you. I needed that." She looked up at him, and he could see that she was still tender. Kissing her lightly on the mouth, he told her that she needed some dinner and that things would look better. Just as they were leaving the store, he came upon a man whom he'd seen before.

He didn't know him at first, only his face. Then, when it came to him, he was surprised to figure out that he'd been turned into a creature of the night. Nodding once at the man, he walked by him and out the door to the awaiting car. They were gone before the man could recognize him.

"Did you know him?" He explained that at one time he'd been a friend. "He didn't look like he is anymore. What happened? Or would you rather not tell me?"

"His name is Ruby Frank. We met one night when I was hungry for a meal, and he was the only one that I could find. This was before I could be out in the sun for any length of time. Anyway, when I fed from him, he had no way of knowing what I was about, so

I took what I needed, left him a little cash, and was on my way. But he remembered me and came to find me." He thought about what the man had wanted from him. "He demanded that I change him into what I was. I have no idea to this day how he found me or what I was. But his demands didn't go unnoticed by the townspeople. Finally, after several weeks of him hounding me, I had to show him my monster, and he finally left me alone. For a time, anyway. I wonder who he got to change him."

"Is that important?" He said that he didn't know, but it must have been someone old, as young vamps usually kill their victims when they try to change them, and he'd been sickly all his life. "So he somehow tricked someone into changing him, and now he's a vampire too. He looked sort of sickly. Like he was suffering from something. I thought that once you were changed, you became a healthy person again."

"That's what I find so weird. He did look like he was sickly, now that you mention it, and he smelled of old blood. Like he's not feeding well, and when he does, it's from the dying." That part was true; they couldn't feed from the dead, or it would likely kill them. He told her that in passing so that she'd know if he ever changed her. "Oh well, I suppose that he's no longer my concern, but I'd like for you to keep an eye out for him. There is no telling what he'd do if he found out you were my mate. I don't know what he'd do, but there is no point in taking the chance. You know his face now, and that's a good thing."

For the rest of the day, they talked about some of the rules that he had to follow, even as an older vampire. There weren't many that he didn't follow, but he was sure that if someone were to go over his life, they'd see that he didn't follow a great many of them. He'd gotten old by his wits, and he wasn't going to change his ways about that and get himself killed at this late in the game. Tabitha seemed to be in a better mood all the way around after the day they'd spent together. He was happy too. It had gotten him out of the house and around others, which was both a good thing and a bad thing. He didn't much care for people as a whole and would just as soon not have to bother with them at all. But he did have his Tabitha, and that was enough for him right now.

Tabitha was nearly standing on her feet, asleep when they got back to Brew's home. After talking with the other couple for a few minutes, telling them of the house that they'd gotten, she went up to bed. He couldn't wait until they shared a room together, even if it was just so he could be near her. But that time would come, and he'd not rush her. She was his world right now, and Sirous was going to do his best to make sure that she was happy with whatever came between them.

He loved her, and that was enough for right now.

Brew and he talked through most of the night. He'd told his best friend that Tabitha had been feeling lonely and explained how that had happened. Brew felt bad for that and said he'd try to refrain from talking solely about vampires from now on, and he appreciated it. He then told him about Ruby.

"I can find out who changed him. It might have been someone that we know, and it'll be easy to get the information. I have access to a lot of things now that I'm getting better at my job. Even Calla is getting better with her magic. But I'll look into it and see what I can find." He said that he didn't know why it was important, but he just felt in his gut that it was. "Then I'll look into it for sure. There is no point in ignoring your gut when it so strongly tells you something. I've learned the hard way about that sort of thing. Don't put it off if you can help it. I'll look into it tomorrow. I promise."

With that promise, he made his way up to bed. He didn't need to rest, but he was reading a good book and wanted to get back to it. He loved to read and was happy that Brew had such an extensive library.

Chapter 6

"He was changed, then he killed his maker." Brew didn't like giving bad news to people, and giving it to his friends was twice as hard. "Ruby wasn't charged because he claimed that he'd not realized that he was going to be starving when he woke up, and that's why he killed him. We're talking a seasoned vampire here. One that had been around a few hundred years, and he didn't warn him that he'd need to be careful? I don't buy that."

"Neither do I. Something else is going on, and I don't like it. Do you know why he's so sickly looking?" He did and told his good friend why. "So he's had some of his magic taken away from him, like glamor. I would imagine that it would be hard to get next to someone when you look like he does. Not to mention the ability to pull shadows. That's the only thing that saved me when I was out looking for someone."

"I don't remember a time when I didn't use shadows around us when we fed. It's the only thing that keeps you safe when you're hungry. No wonder he's only drinking from the dying. If he gets too much of that blood, he's going to end up getting himself killed

one day. That's a dangerous sort of habit to get into."
Sirous agreed with him and then asked him who had
changed him. "Donald McGee. You might remember
him being on the council at one point. I don't think he
lasted all that long, but he did make some changes that
are still around to this day. Like the money we give
to the council for vamps that are struggling. That's
helped a great many younger vamps who think that
money just comes to them when they're turned."

"They also think they're going to be good-
looking as well. I knew one vamp that had been
changed, and she thought that she was going to be
younger-looking and thinner. That only happens if
when you change and you looked like that before."
They both had come from a long line of vampires
and didn't have those issues. They would stop aging
around the time they turned twenty-five. Not even
their hair grew longer after that. It was as if everything
stopped, and they would look as they did at that age.
Or in the case of the vampire that Brew knew, when
she'd been changed.

"What do you want to do about this? I don't
know the man other than what I've read about him, so
this would be in your ballpark." He told him that he
didn't know just yet, but he didn't believe for a moment
that he'd killed his maker by accident. "I don't either.
But what do we do about it?"

"I guess nothing for now. But can you keep an eye on him? Just to see if there are any more unexplained deaths surrounding him? I have a feeling that he's been making the rules up as he goes along." Brew asked him what he meant. "Pulling out the rules as they suit him. And when they don't, he suddenly doesn't remember that one being told to him. I have a feeling that there is going to be a string of bodies attached to this guy when you start digging."

"I will because I trust your gut as well as I do my own." He pulled up the information on Ruby and told Sirous what he'd been able to find. "The two deaths that have been reported are just as you said he'd say. He'd not been told of those kinds of rules, so he couldn't be prosecuted because of them. What new or even, for that matter, old vampire doesn't know all the rules? They're force-fed to us from birth. And if you're changed, don't you have to sign something that says you read over the rules that govern us?"

"Yes, and I have it signed right here. Good thought that one." He laid the report next to his computer and pulled out other paperwork from the file. "He's been in trouble with the council before. Something about making money by talking to humans about vampires. I think he was talking to some author who was writing a romance book about our kind, and it got around."

"Those books have saved us a great deal when it comes to us blending in. I don't know how many times, when I was younger, eating garlic has gotten me overlooked." He shivered then. "Nasty tasting stuff if you ask me, but it worked. Then there is the no reflection issue that's simply not true. How would we even know how we looked when we left the house if we couldn't see what we looked like? Do you suppose he's feeding this person lies to keep our kind safe?"

"He can't be both good and bad, and I think you know that." Sirous said he knew that but didn't want to jump to conclusions about anyone. "I'll keep an eye on him and see what we can find out. If he's just selling information that's not true, there isn't much I can do about that. But the rest, his selling true information will get his ass killed. And I'd be the one to do it to him."

"Thanks. I don't know why I have a feeling about him being in trouble, but if the little bit you've found out now is true, there is no reason not to believe that he's not doing anything else wrong as well." Brew made some notes on the man and decided that he was going to do a deep dive into his life. It couldn't hurt, and if he didn't find out anything, no one would be the wiser. He told Sirous that he had it covered. "I know you do. I already feel better with you on the case."

After Sirous left him, he began working on

the file. There were some petty things that he'd been doing, but nothing that anyone else hadn't been up to since being a vampire. Just as he was ready to close the file on the man for now, he saw a note from the council that talked about looking into his life as well. He decided to get with them to see what he could find out.

It didn't take him long to get with the three of them. There used to be five on the council, but when one of them retired, one of the ones left had to be fired. There could only be an odd number of people on the board, and he liked just having three of them. Much easier to get with them when you wanted them around, and they seemed to get along better, too. He asked about Ruby, and they knew who he was talking about. Not a good start for the man, he thought.

"We've been keeping an eye on him as best we could. There are times when we get busy and forget about him for decades at a time, but we get back around to it when he's done something that will gather our attention." He asked what that was the last time. "He claimed that the man he'd been living with had taken liberties, but he'd never say what they were. He'd killed him one night in a rage after the man had done this. He claimed that to repeat it gave him nightmares, and he wasn't sleeping well at all. But the thing is, he left him all his money when he passed on, and we found that to be suspicious. He'd been left a great deal of money from another source, too, that we couldn't find any wrongdoing of."

"Why haven't I heard about this before? I could have had one of the faeries looking after him to see if we have a pattern. Though it sounds like we do anyway." Brew listened to their complaints about being overworked, and there were just too many easy cases that they could solve. "So, just because this one is hard, you decided that it wasn't worth your time to look into it. Is that what you're saying?"

"Pretty much. If you knew the workload that we had, you'd be exhausted too. Why, just the other week I almost didn't get my time off from being too busy here to make the time." Brew had no idea why, but he could almost fire the lot of them. "We get a lot of easy cases in our hands that we solve. And restitution is done immediately. That's the way that most of the other vampires like it."

"Well, I don't, and since I'm king, I want the harder cases done as they come in. There will be no more vacation time unless I approve it. And that's only after you show me how you've worked on some of the harder cases to have them resolved." He said that he couldn't do that. "Oh, but I can. As king, I can have all of you fired and bring in a crew that I hand-picked. Then I'll be looking into what you've done around here to see if there are some disciplinary actions that need to be taken out against you three."

"We get things done around here. Why, just yesterday, I got three of the easy ones resolved, and the money was paid to the vampire in question, minus our fee. We take a little off the top in order to have enough money to live. None of us has had a pay raise in decades. If you were a better king, you would have figured that out while you were looking into Ruby Frank's life. I told you that we looked into things and didn't find anything at the time."

"It's the 'at the time' that bothers me. I wonder what else he's been up to when you're not looking. Do you perhaps tell him when you're looking into his life?" They said that was one of the rules that they followed. A person needed to be notified that they were being investigated. "Show me that rule. I want to see how it's worded."

None of them could produce the rule on paper or in any other form. Then he was told it was easier to watch him when he wasn't doing anything wrong. Christ, he wanted to kill the lot of them before he left, but he wasn't going to do that. He needed them there for now. But he was going to find someone that he trusted to do the paperwork on vamps if it was the last thing he did.

After dismissing them, he sent three faeries on

Ruby without his knowledge. Of course, it would be easier to watch someone if they were being on their best behavior. He'd bet anything, too, that he was told when they were finished with the investigation as well. And he was sure that it didn't last all that long either. They'd watch for a couple of days, hell, even a couple of hours, and when he didn't do anything, he'd be able to go right back to what he'd been doing before. If they did that to every case that came in, it's small wonder anyone was fined or arrested who had been wrong-doing. He didn't understand why they'd bothered to take away some of his magic if he wasn't doing anything wrong. Well, he was going to take care of it today if he had to work all night to get it done. For now, however, he was going to keep it to himself on what was going on so that he could catch the young vamp at something he shouldn't be doing.

It was nearly midnight when he had all the information that he needed on Ruby to take care of him. He'd been buying up insurance policies on humans, then killing them off. It had taken him a bit of effort to find his method on how he would kill them off, but once he had that, it was only a matter of finding unsolved deaths that had to do with carjackings. Several hundred of them appeared, and Ruby's name was on all the policies that had been taken out. Christ, the man was making a million dollars a month by using his scheme.

Calling Sirous to him, he was glad that he was able to let him know what was going on. The very fact that he'd been implicated in a lot of the deaths by the humans notwithstanding, he was not on his list. Sirous figured that once he killed the people who had tried to hijack his car, he would drink from them while they were dying. He couldn't collect on their policies if they lived, so by drinking from them while they were near death, he would ensure that they didn't make it to another carjacking. And since he did it all over the United States, it was difficult for any one police officer to be able to put two and two together to get a scam.

"I have enough to prove that he's doing it now, but I'm going to have the faeries watching him. Not that I want another death, but as soon as he takes out a policy on someone, then I'm going to bring him in for questioning. I'll have him by the end of the week for sure." Sirous thanked him for looking so deeply into it. "That's what gives our kind such a bad name. All this could have been avoided if the council would have gotten off their asses and killed him before now. I mean, he's been doing this for the last three decades or so. Someone should have caught him at it well before now."

"I agree. I'll help you in any way that you need me to do." He asked him if he knew of anyone who could serve on the council board. "I don't off the top of my head, but I'll keep that in mind. I don't want it. I've only just found my mate, and that sounds like it would take up too much of my time."

"It would. Especially with the backlog they have now." He told his good friend how they were only doing the easy cases. "I should remove their heads and be done with it. I do wonder if the faeries would be any good at it? It's something to think about, isn't it?"

"I should think they'd be happy to have the job." Brew was warming to the idea the longer he talked to Sirous. "I can look into that for you. They'd have it all done in about a week if you were to have them start on them now."

"I'm going to ask someone if they can do it. You look into it as well." He was mentally rubbing his hands together, thinking of a way that they could get it finished up. "Yes, I think that this will be the best way to rid ourselves of the council we have now and have things up to date too."

~*~

Ruby had been playing the victim for so long that he was getting sick of it. He wanted to branch out and become a king, but knew that once he did that, he'd never have any time to make any money when he wanted. He'd be on display all the time, and that wouldn't get him a lick of work done. He liked playing the role he thought that he'd been born to.

Standing in line to collect on his latest victim, someone that he barely knew but had needed money, he thought about how he'd perfected the plan that he'd been working on since he'd been carjacked once a long time ago. The man had been desperate to get to the hospital to see his wife give birth to his child that he'd nearly killed Ruby when he'd tossed him out of the car to take it. That didn't end well for the man, and sadly, he never got to see his newborn baby being born or anything to do with his life. Ruby had broken his neck when he'd taken his car.

It had been too easy for him to just take out the policies on the people that he claimed had wronged him. Sometimes it was just too easy for him to make the kind of money that he did. He'd thought about writing a book on the way to do it, but then that would guarantee two things. He'd get caught, and there would be so many people doing it that it wouldn't work as well as it was right now. Besides, he was just too lazy to write anything down other than his name on policies, and that was the truth of the matter. Being lazy had its advantages as well. He never had to work very hard at anything.

Collecting on the latest victim, he nearly left without making sure that he deposited just enough to keep his account open. The bank wouldn't cash his checks without an account at the bank, so he had to spend some of his winnings—just what he called his new scam—in the bank.

He hated to save the account and have it stay open, but it was the only way that he could get what he wanted and still be able to have some fun. And fun he did have too. This latest scam was netting him over a million dollars a month, so long as he was careful.

He made sure that his victims weren't that close to each other. He'd been all over the United States playing his scam, and so far, he'd never been caught. He supposed that it was because he was smarter than the average person and knew how to make it work. He'd been doing this particular scam for the past three decades, and so far, no one was the wiser. Then there was the council.

A stupider trio of people that he'd ever met. They would actually tell him when they were going to keep an eye on him because he'd told them that was a rule. It had been a chance that he took with them, and so far it had worked. Not only did they tell him when they were looking into what he'd been up to, but they would tell him when they were finished. Like he thought, they were too stupid to hold such a high office for the amount of work they had to be doing.

"Ruby James Frank?" He told the little faerie that was his name. "My name is Winter, I'm a faerie to the king of vampires. He wishes to see you. Now."

He found himself in a different place than he'd been before. Looking around, he couldn't believe that he was in a home. The man standing in front of him didn't look happy. Well, neither was he. But he wasn't going to say anything to get himself into trouble. There was no reason for him to be taken from his day to come here.

"What is the meaning of this? I was going to be finding myself some work today and —"

"Do shut up before I make it so that you can't talk at all." The man had a lot of nerve, but Ruby decided that he'd let him hang himself by trying to talk terribly to him. He wasn't used to people treating him with such disdain. "Now, I'm going to talk to you about your killing humans for profit. You've been taking out policies on them and then killing them for the past thirty years."

"I don't know what you're talking about. You'll have to explain." He told him how he'd been watching him for the past several weeks and had found his information to be true. "Watching over me? You can't do that unless you notify me of it. I know the rules."

"So do I, and there is no such rule regarding warning you when you're going to be observed." He knew there wasn't, but didn't know that the man would know too. "Also, you've been seen taking money from the dying so that you can profit that way as well. There are plenty of rules that say that you cannot steal from humans while they lie dying. Especially when you're the one who caused their deaths. What do you have to say about that?"

"Who are you to say such slanderous things about me?" He told him who he was. "I don't know anything about you being king of vampires. You're making that up."

"It was felt by all vampires the day that I was chosen to do the job. You would have been told who I was and that I was going to rule from now on." He said there must have been something wrong with him that day, and he'd not known about it. "Lies will get you nowhere, Ruby Frank. But you will manage to piss me off even more. You'll be sentenced directly unless you have a good reason for what you've done to the human race."

"I don't know what you're talking about." He'd gotten away with that before and thought that this man was just stupid enough to believe him. But if his face was any indication, he wasn't buying it. "Look, there's been a misunderstanding about this. I'll just go back to where I was if you'd allow it and not do this thing again. I'll even find myself a respectable job and work for the money that I need."

"You will be killed on the spot where you stand

now." He saw the large claw-like hand reach out for him, and he couldn't move. Instead of slicing through his body as he had assumed that he would, he simply pushed his long nails into his flesh and let him bleed. "You will suffer with this wound for all time until such time that you die. I have spoken."

He found himself where he'd been before and weaker than he'd ever been in his life. As he was trying to walk back to his lair, he stumbled twice and nearly fell. This was ridiculous. Why was he being treated this way all of a sudden when he'd gotten by with so much before? He was going to have to appeal to the council and see what they had to say. He'd been talking to the three of them for decades, and he'd been able to get by with a great deal. Now, all of a sudden, he was in trouble with the king of his kind.

"Damn it, this wasn't fair." He wasn't ready to quit his profit-making deal. It was too much money to just give up on a whim of some man claiming to be King. "I'm not going to bleed to death either. That's just a stupid notion. He can't just say something and have it happen."

But he had a feeling that was just what was going to happen was just as he'd been told. He had too much to do in this life for it to be taken right now. He was going to have to do something before he died unfairly.

He'd always been weak in the first place. He knew that it was because he'd been drinking from the dying, but he saw no reason to let all that good blood go to waste. Plus, since losing his ability to use shadows, it was keeping him from drinking from humans when he needed to. Then there was the reason that he thought that humans should want to feed his kind. We were far more superior to them than any other race, he thought.

He was weak by the time he got back to his lair. It was just an abandoned building on the outskirts of town. It was perfect for his needs, and he saw no reason to waste money on fine hotels or even a house when he could spend his money on other things, like fine paintings and good art. He had a collection worthy of a king—he had to laugh about his pun and decided that the king didn't have as much fine art as he did. What was going to happen to his collection when he died? Nothing because he wasn't going to die, and that was final.

Resting during the hottest part of the day, he hated that he wasn't old enough to forgo that; he woke to a bed covered in his blood. While he could clean it up easily enough, he was too weak to do anything more than to leave it until later. The man had really done a number on him, and he wasn't the least bit happy about it.

By the time the night was over for him and the

sun was coming up, he could barely walk to the couch to lie down; he was so weak. This wasn't fair, and he was going to tell someone about his treatment as soon as he was strong enough to get up and get going. He was beginning to think that he was surely going to die, and for what? He'd done nothing wrong. He'd always believed that humans were there for their pleasure, and he hadn't changed his mind on that in all the years that he'd been turned into a vampire.

He remembered fondly the day he'd been turned. Not wanting anyone else to know that he'd been changed, he killed his maker. It had been much easier than he thought it should have been, him newly turned and all. However, his maker hadn't been that much older than he was at the time, and it had surprised them both; he thought that he'd been able to slice open his throat and be finished with him.

Laughing just a little, his body was beginning to hurt some, so he decided that he'd do well to take another nap and try to get some rest. He usually felt better after his nap during the evening hours, and he hoped that today was no different.

His fitful rest did him no good. Again, he woke covered in blood and decided that he was truly going to die today. All he could think about was the unfairness of it all and how he'd been made to do the things he'd done because no one had shared the rules with him.

Laughing again, he thought that wasn't right. He knew the real rules better than most. Knowing them was what had gotten him into all the things that he'd been into because knowing them is how he was able to work around them. He wasn't as stupid as anyone thought he was.

Unable to drag himself up and off the couch, he was surprised to see Winter again. She was saying something to him about the king going to inherit his worth, and he didn't like that either. Of course, as weak as he was, there was little to nothing he could do about it, so he just laid there while his things disappeared one at a time from his walls and floor.

"Those are my treasures that I paid for with my own money." Again, Winter spoke to him, but he couldn't make out what he was saying. Something about humans again, and he didn't have the strength to answer him. "This is so unfair, you understand? I have these things here so that it doesn't look so dreary. It's my stuff."

"You own nothing." She was close enough that he could have snatched her right out of the air, but he couldn't lift his hand. "You're ready to die now. Do you have any last words?"

"Why me? Why was I singled out over anyone else?" He said that he was a monster to the humans, and that was why he was targeted. "I don't believe that I've done anything wrong. I don't deserve this. I demand that you allow me to live on with my life as I see fit."

"Nay, you are the monster that small children have nightmares about. That is not meant as a compliment either. You have done them wrong by taking their fathers and mothers away. Humans don't deserve to be treated as cattle, nor are they there for your entertainment." He couldn't form words and knew that he was at the end of his life. One that he'd enjoyed until the king had gotten a burr up his ass about him. "When you die, no one will ever remember your name, nor will they care a bit that you've gone. Goodbye, Ruby James Frank. Your life is at its end."

The pain was too much as he was turned to ash. He didn't deserve this and would tell anyone who would listen to him in the afterlife. However, just then, he thought that there would be no afterlife for him. He'd royally screwed up, and there would be nothing of him left.

Chapter 7

Sirous needed to feed. It didn't happen often, but this time he'd gone too far in letting himself get too hungry. He was either going to convince Tabitha that he needed to feed from her or find someone else to feed from, and that didn't suit him. Nor did he think that it would suit Tabitha for him to be smelling like someone else. If she cared at all.

"What's wrong with you?" He bowed before her and told her what was going on. "I've told you before that I was willing to allow you to feed from me. Why did you wait so long to do it? Is your need that powerful?" He said that he'd sadly made a mistake about how long it had been, and now he was afraid to start with her. "You mean because of the sex thing, too? Or is it something else? Whatever it is, I trust you."

"It's the sex thing." He wasn't making fun of her, but he didn't know what else to do. If she turned him away now, he was going to have to find a willing partner and feed from them. "I promised you that I wouldn't force you, and this will seem as though I have. I'm sorry."

"Don't be sorry. Just don't wait so long until you

need to feed again." She looked at him and frowned. "Do we have to call it feeding? It sounds like you're an animal at the zoo or something, and I'm going to have to toss food at you to make you not hangry. That's a word I believe."

"I'm not hangry at all, just hungry." He looked at the pounding pulse in her throat and could hear her heart beating quickly. "I would only need a sip or two, but I want you as well. I don't want to break a promise to you, but I fear that I might take more than you're willing to give me."

"I'm willing to give you my all. I told you that I've fallen in love with you, and I have. I don't know why I've been waiting all this time, but now that we're so close, I find that I'm a little afraid of you. No one has ever bitten me during sex. Will it hurt?" He told her only for a moment before she had her first of many climaxes. "All right then, take what you need."

"I fear for you." She told him that she wasn't worried about him hurting her. "I fear that I might take too much and harm you in some way. I don't want to do that."

"Then don't. You won't hurt me. I believe that with all my heart." She sat down on the couch, then leaned back against the back of it, baring her throat for him. It was all he could do not to pounce on her and take all of her. But he knew that would scare her, and he didn't want to do that. Getting on the couch beside her, he made sure that he was in a position to take her and not harm her. "I trust you, Sirous. I have for a long time. Just bite me and take what you need so that you can be as strong as you need to be. I have fallen in love with you, and I trust you."

He hoped that she wasn't giving him too much credit with her trust. He wanted her to enjoy him taking from her, but he also knew that he could easily harm her. Cursing himself for waiting for so long, he kissed her gently on the mouth before making his way down her chin to her throat. He could almost smell the essence of her blood then.

Biting gently into her flesh, he nearly came himself when he tasted the first few drops of her blood. Drinking deeply, he could taste her magic around her and knew too that there had been several vampires in her lineage. Drinking deeply, careful to listen to her heart beating, he pulled at her clothing until her pussy was naked for him. He could smell her there, too. She was so wet that she soaked his fingers when he touched her womanhood.

Her release took his breath away. She came so prettily that he wanted to taste her pussy far more than he wanted to drink from her throat. Sealing the wound at her neck, he made his way down to her juncture and inhaled deeply. He wanted her all.

"Are you going to feed from me there?" Christ, he was dizzy with the idea of what she'd suggested. Getting down on the floor, he pulled her pants off the rest of the way and tossed them across the room. Opening her legs, he was salivating; he could almost taste the treasures that she had. Opening her nether lips up, he suckled her clit into his mouth and bit down.

Blood and cream filled him. Her scream of a climax had him drinking deeply of her again and again. Sliding his finger deep inside of her, he gathered more of her cream while he suckled hard on her. With every deep drink he took, he felt his body filling out more on her special blood. Christ, he was going to come now, but knew that he needed to give her more of himself. He wanted to see her face when he took her and was glad that the room was brightly lit so that he could. Never was he going to take her in the darkness of the night when he could see all that she offered him during the day.

Even as he fucked her with his fingers and tongue, she flooded his mouth with more of her. He sealed the wound but didn't stop from drinking from her. The essences that she was feeding him would last a great deal longer than her blood would have, and he found that he didn't want to stop. Bringing her over and over, she was weak with his fucking of her, and he didn't care. And it seemed neither did she. One moment she'd be begging him to stop, and the next she would beg him for more.

Looking up from his position on the floor, he could see that she'd taken off her blouse, and her bra was pushed up under her chin. What she was doing to her nipples made him stare at her for several moments as his cock got harder still. He wanted to suckle at her nipples, feed from them. Leaning his head toward her breasts, Tabitha held them out to him like an offering, and he couldn't help but to take what she offered him.

Fucking her with his fingers and taking her nipples deep into his mouth, he wanted to fuck her hard enough to bring them both over the edge. The thought of being buried deep inside of her nearly had him growling low at her when she pulled his hair up from his feast.

"Take me. I need to come." He growled again.

He let a little of himself go and jerked her over so that her ass was just over the couch. Running his hand down the muscled flesh, he licked a path from the back of her neck to her ass. That was when he slid behind her and slammed his cock deep inside of her pussy. His eyes rolled to the back of his head, and he could see stars. Fucking her harder now, not thinking about her pleasure, he came twice. Nothing to satisfy him but enough where he could finally see what he was doing. And hearing her cries of pleasure had him digging his nails deep within her flesh and holding on while he fucked her.

When he was nearing his climax again, he pulled her hair up from the cushion and held her there while he bit down hard on her throat. When her spiced blood filled his mouth, he came roaring around her neck as he filled her with his cum. Nothing could have prepared him for the second time he came when he passed out on top of her.

Waking, it had only been a few moments, he thought, he held her to him as he kissed his way down her back. She was going to be bruised for sure, but he found that he liked the thought of her wearing his marks. Turning her over, he was frightened when she was so limp. But he could hear her heart beating and feel her breaths. He'd hurt her, he thought, and would never forgive himself if she never wanted to have sex with him again.

"That was fantastic." He looked into her eyes to see if she was all right. "You can feed from me every day if you do it like that. I've never come so hard in my life."

"I thought that I'd hurt you." Tabitha said she was sore right now, but nothing would make her unhappy with the number of times that she'd come. "You were passed out."

"I did. I loved it." He wasn't one to seek

compliments when he made love to a woman, but today he needed reassurances like never before. When she rolled to her back and put her hands on his face, he could feel her love for him as if it were a physical thing. Kissing her palm, he told her how much he'd enjoyed it too and was looking forward to fucking her again. "That was fucking, wasn't it. And for as much as I enjoyed that, I'm looking forward to you simply making love to me, too. I bet you can be gentle when the time is right. I hope that sometime you show me your beast so that I can thank him for a good time."

Her giggle had him smiling. When her eyes closed for a moment, he thought that she was resting. Staring at her face, seeing a beauty there that he'd not seen before, Sirous counted himself the luckiest man on earth. Picking up his mate, who never stirred, he made his way up to the bedroom she'd been using and put her on the mattress. It took him several tries to get the blankets pulled down correctly, but all in all, he was proud of himself. He'd not dropped her once.

Feeling the power of her blood filling him, he knew that he'd get no sleep beside her. Instead, he brought over a chair and sat watching her sleep. Her breath was sweet-smelling, and he could see that she was completely relaxed, so he didn't bother her with touching her face. He wanted her to be rested when she woke again.

Sirous was in love with his little mate. He'd thought he'd been before, loving her because she was his, but he knew that this love, the one that he was feeling now, was the kind that lasted forever. The one kind of love that would take them through the good times and bad. Though at the moment, he couldn't think of a single thing that would come to them that he'd consider bad. He was so in love with Tabitha that he wanted to find someone, anyone, and tell them what he was feeling for the woman who would stay with him throughout eternity.

Going to his office so he'd not do something stupid like wake her to tell her what he was feeling, he sat behind his computer and focused all his energy on what was there. He had some investments to make and some money to move around so that his charities could get what they needed. The longer he sat there, the more he got done. It was like loving his mate had given him a bit more energy than he'd ever had, and he was happy for it.

They were going to be moving into their forever home in the morning. All the things that they'd purchased were going to be delivered in the afternoon. Plenty of time for them to get things situated, like paintings on the wall and the little knick-knacks that they purchased to put in the rooms that they would be shown off in.

Even the kitchen was going to have a touch of art in it just because he knew that they'd be spending a great deal of time in there. He had been told by Brew that watching his mate eat was sexy, and he decided that he wasn't going to miss a moment of any time he could be around her. When Brew reached out to him, he couldn't help but tell him how much he loved his mate.

"I know just what you're saying. I can't stand to be a moment away from my own mate unless I'm driving her crazy. Even then, I want to be there next to her." He said that she was sleeping now and he'd had to make himself leave her alone so as not to keep waking her to tell her how he felt. *"You'll have to find ways to show her how much you love her. I've been finding ways to make her smile so that I can know that I'm the one who put that look on her face."*

"I have all this energy too. I feel as if I might explode if I don't do something productive." Neither one mentioned having sex with Tabitha, but he was sure that's what Brew was thinking. *"You must think that I'm silly. What is it you wanted me for?"*

"Oh. I have taken care that Ruby is dead. I let his death linger a bit so that I could find where he was staying. If he'd been in a cave around here, there wouldn't have been any way that I could have found him. However, he was staying in a house on the outskirts of town, and I've found what he's

been doing with the money. You're to have your share of his bounty for your help in this. Also, I've dismissed the council. Had they done their job, he wouldn't have killed as many *people, humans as he'd been allowed to.*" He said that he didn't need the money. "*There is no money, believe it or not, but artwork that he's been collecting. It's some beautiful pieces that will look lovely in your new home. I've taken a couple of pieces for my work in getting him out of the human population, but the rest, and there is a great deal of it, will go to you.*"

"*Art? I have some pieces myself that we're going to hang. It'll look lovely in the new home as you said.*" Brew told him that there were over one hundred pieces that would be coming to him. "*I'll hang it in the guest rooms. They'll never believe that I have such pieces just hanging around.*"

"*I have one that I put in the half bath downstairs. It's the perfect match to the things already in there, and like you said, no one would think I'd be stupid enough to put it in a bathroom of all places.*" They both laughed, and Sirous asked him when they were going to be delivered. "*Most of the pieces have already been delivered to your home. You need only find a place to hang them when you get there. The rest will be given to you after you've moved in. It's mostly sculptures and the like. That way, they won't get broken while you're moving things in.*"

"*I'll take it. And whatever I can't use, I'll give to the*

others. I'm sure that once they find their houses, they'd like to have some work in their homes as well." He'd have to find something special for Yosef. He'd made it so that he found his mate. *"I'll make sure that they understand where it came from, too. Was any of it stolen?"*

"No, he bought it all. As he laid dying, he said to Winter that it was in the abandoned house so that it would be less dreary. I wondered why he didn't buy a house to put them in, but I didn't think to ask him." Sirous thought that the man was stupid for putting works of art in an abandoned home, but he had been killing humans, too. He had to know that he was going to get caught sometime. *"I'll talk to you later tomorrow. I have a couple of meetings in the morning with the committee that is taking care of the school bus fund. We'll be matching it dollar for dollar in what they get."*

"Good luck with that." After closing the connection, he went to check on Tabitha and found that she was still sleeping. Now that he'd gotten rid of a burst of the energy that he had, he laid down beside her. Sirous was out within seconds and knew that he had a smile on his face.

~*~

Tabby woke in the big bed without knowing how she'd gotten there. Not really too worried about it, she sat up in the bed and looked around. She was excited to be sharing the big room with Sirous now and was happy that they'd finally made love. Going to the bathroom, she could feel every one of her muscles protesting movement, and she nearly sobbed with relief when she finally got to the room.

There were bruises all over her body. But almost as soon as she found them, they disappeared quickly. Even her feet were sore, and she couldn't for the life of her figure out why. As she turned on the hot water for a nice, long hot shower, she tried reaching out to Sirous to find out where he was in the house. She found him in the living room with the delivery people, and that's how she knew that she'd slept round the clock to the next morning.

"I was wondering if you were going to wake soon. I was thinking that I was going to have to call out for you when the furniture arrived." She said she must have needed the sleep. *"I slept with you for a while. I was a little sore before I took a shower. How are you feeling?"*

"The same. Sore. I've thought that taking a shower would help. So far, I'm finding more aches and pains to go with the ones that I had when I woke up." He told her how sorry he was. *"I'm not, and you shouldn't be either. We had a wonderful time and I don't regret a moment of it."*

"You're so right. We did have a good time." She felt his smile and was glad for it. When she finally turned off the water to the shower, she did feel better. Getting dressed with the magic that she had, she was

downstairs just as the last of the furniture was taken off the truck. She was so excited to have their home finished out that she realized that she'd slept in the new house without knowing it. She asked Sirous about that. "I brought you here this morning. I wanted you to be able to wake up in our new home after yesterday. Christ, you were amazing."

He kissed her then, and she kissed him back. She was so in love with the big vampire that she didn't know what to do with it all. Give it back to him, she thought, and was happy when she was able to hug him.

For the rest of the morning, they moved furniture around. They actually used magic to move it around in the rooms, but it was still exhausting. As soon as the living room was finished with the paintings hung on the walls, they laid down on one of their couches and closed their eyes. As they were in no hurry to finish up, they decided a nap would be perfect. The two of them woke when someone came to the door. It was Brew and the rest of the men to help out with moving things around.

"We've all but finished." They looked so disappointed that Sirous laughed. "I suppose you can help us unpack the kitchen items. There are a lot of boxes that need to be broken down as well. That would be a tremendous help to us. And we'll order in dinner for you guys."

It took no time at all to get the kitchen finished. Their cook started tomorrow—she was from the pack that roamed the land, and she had already given them a list of staples that she'd need to start cooking for her. She was excited to have her own cook so she'd not have to prepare anything, but was sad because Sirous wouldn't be able to join her.

"Oh, but I plan on watching you eat every meal." She asked him why he'd do that. "Because my dearest, I have a feeling watching you eat a meal will be just the motivation that I need to want to take you against the counters."

"Oh." She thought about that off and on all day and wondered why it never occurred to her that he'd do something like that. She was going to have to think of ways to eat food more sexily and entice him to take her anywhere he wanted her. By the time dinner was being delivered, she'd thought of several ways she could eat pizza and get him going. But not tonight. They had too much in the way of company, and that wouldn't do for them to run off to the bedroom while the others were around.

Giggling to herself, she knew that she was going to have fun living in a house by themselves. They'd been living in Brew's home with Calla, so they had to have respect for their privacy, too. Shivering a little in anticipation, she wondered what they'd do after everyone left tonight. Break in the new bed, perhaps? She didn't care; she wanted some fun with her mate.

As it turned out, they didn't leave until well after two in the morning. She knew that it was because they were used to staying up all night, but she was too exhausted to wait up for Sirous. He was having fun with the others, and she couldn't blame him for that. Once she went up to bed, she took a long, hot shower and got into bed. Hopefully, going to bed naked would clue Sirous in on how she was feeling.

Turns out that didn't work either, as he never came to bed that night. Frustrated, she went down to breakfast and ate without him. She was being petty for sure, but at this point, she didn't care. He was neglecting his duties to her, and she was getting sick of it. Then she laughed to herself. Duties? The man had thousands of years on her, and they had thousands more before they were finished. She couldn't begrudge him one night without making love to him.

Feeling better about herself, she wished then that she'd waited on Sirous. The man was still hanging out with his friends when she was finished with her meal. Going to see what they had planned for the day, she was surprised to find that they were alone in the big house. Asking him what had happened, he smiled at her. She couldn't resist him when he was in a good mood and sat down beside him on the couch.

"I sent them on their way. I didn't realize that we'd been together all night again until the sun was coming up and I heard you in the kitchen. I missed breakfast with you." She told him she'd only had a bowl of cereal, so he didn't miss much. "But I did miss sleeping with you. I shant do that again. I love waking up to your warm body wrapped around mine. It's the highlight of my day."

"You're goofy." They both laughed, and she realized how much she'd been doing that lately. Just laughing because she wasn't as stressed out as she'd been. "Calla told me that the judge is coming through town in the morning, and my mother will have her hearing. I guess he could fine her and let her go. I hope not. I've been enjoying being around the town without her right on my heels. And I like not having her hounding me for money all the time. Do you suppose she'll get out?"

"It's hard to say what will happen. She's not done anything wrong but to harass you. I don't believe she's been the one who has physically beaten you up, has she?" She told him not of late. "It's really hard to know what the judge will do. I'd throw the book at her, but that's just me. I'm hoping that she gets up there and claims that you can give her the racing scores so that she looks like a fool. It's going to be obvious to the judge that you have no need for such magic, and he might send her off to be tested for her sanity. I'm hoping that he does that. That'll put her out of commission for a bit longer. If they find her insane, then she'll go away. I'm hoping anyway."

"So you're saying that I should play dumb when she claims that I can do that." He said it would go a long way in her being insane. "I'll do it. I've been saying that I can't do the things I can do for a while now, so that won't be a bother. I just hope she doesn't get out to bother me again. I was wondering if the burin can hold her responsible for the death of Carl. He only did what she told him to do, and that's what got him into trouble."

"That's a good thought. I should see what he wants to do with that information." She said that she'd heard about it from a wolf pack once when they were being influenced by a group of humans. The pack master found them guilty of the crimes that the pack had been committing, and they were all fined a great deal of money because of the loss of their income when they had to be put to death. I think there was actual murder involved, but I'm not sure about all the details."

"It's something to ask about." He wrapped his arms around her, and she snuggled up against him. "It's going to be a long day today. I should have sent them all home earlier so that I could get some rest. You've worn me out."

"I guess you're too tired to make love to me again." He said never and wiggled his brows at her. "You really are a different man than the one that I met so long ago, it seems. I really like this version of you."

"I do as well. I feel lighter than before. I'm certainly sleeping when I need to much better. Not to mention, I'm feeling better with you around. It's like I've been given a second chance at life and I'm enjoying it again. And all because of you." He kissed her on the forehead and held her tightly against him. She loved this part of the man she was mated to because he was so generous with his affections. "How about we go upstairs and you lie down with me while I nap. Then, when I wake up, it shouldn't be but a couple of hours, I'll make love to you like you deserve. Slow and sweet."

She didn't even care if they made love at this point, so long as he was with her. They'd been making love, both rough and sweet, for the last several days, both in the morning and in the evening. If she were honest with herself, she would say that she was worn out, too, and needed a nap, but didn't. He would go to the ends of the earth for her to be relaxed enough to sleep, and she just wanted to be held by him for a bit.

Life had taken on a new look for her. She'd been so depressed before about her mother and Carl that she didn't want to go on living either. It would have been easier for her to allow him to end her life so that she'd be all right. Never in her life had she been so happy that she wanted to live more with each passing day.

As they laid down in the big bed, she worried that she'd not be able to rest. Just as she was thinking she was going to keep Sirous awake and him not get his rest, she heard him breathe a single word over her. Sleep. Her entire body relaxed then, and she closed her eyes. Whatever magic he used on her, it had worked. She was asleep in no time at all.

Chapter 8

Linda didn't know what she'd been arrested for, nor did she care at this point. She had things to do, and she wasn't getting anything done concerning her daughter. The bitch had thralled her for the last time. She wanted money, and she wanted a great deal of it. Tomorrow, she was going before a judge about how she'd been threatening her own child. She knew that there were laws about threatening people, but she didn't believe that it covered children. People threatened their kids all the time with punishment, and she'd never seen one of them arrested.

"I wish they made a book of laws that you're not supposed to do. That would be helpful." She'd been told before there were plenty of books on how not to get into trouble with the law, but for the life of her, she couldn't figure out where to find it. Not that she'd read the thing, but it would be nice to have one so that she could mark the ones that she wanted to discard. "Why are there so many supposed laws about hurting your children and nothing about children treating their parents with disdain? That's what I'd like to know."

"You're talking to yourself again." She didn't

know who the man was that was down from her in the cells, but he must have been a pain in the ass as to what got him in jail. He was forever pointing things out that she'd do, and it was getting on her last nerve. "Why don't you talk to yourself lower so I don't have to listen to your stupidity. You sound like a fool when you talk about laws and such. Just know that there are laws about everything that you do wrong. I'm reasonably sure that you can tell when you're doing something wrong, can't you?"

"Mind your own business. I don't talk to you when you mess up." So far, she'd not been able to tell when he did anything wrong, but that was beside the point. She didn't like him talking to her, and she really didn't care for him pointing out the things that she did wrong. In his opinion, she was a total screw, and she knew better. She'd gotten along in life pretty well so far, and she didn't like being pointed at when she might mess up. Stupid bastard needed his head bashed in. And yeah, she knew that was wrong of her to think about. "Fucking bastard."

He said something else, but she was focused on the fact that the door down the hall from the two of them had opened. She'd been telling the cops around here that she wanted to talk to her daughter for days now, and she was hoping they finally got it into their heads that she wasn't joking about it. Tabby owed her, and she was going to come through, or she was going to have someone kill her. That was final too. If she wouldn't help her, then she didn't deserve to live.

It was someone who had come and stopped at her cell, but she didn't know who she was. It took her several minutes of her staring at the girl to know that it was her Tabby. She looked like she glowed a bit. Or she was in love. She'd heard that she was shacked up with some man and wouldn't have believed it but for just then. Christ, even her clothing was expensive-looking.

"I see you've been spending my money on yourself. That's not going to work for me. Tomorrow, when I'm given a bail amount, you're going to pay it without a word of meanness and not give me any shit about how it's not right that you can see the ponies." She told her that she didn't know what she was talking about. "You do too know what I'm saying. I'm not going to have you making me look like a fool when we get before the judge. You're going to tell him what you can do, and you're going to get me my money when I get out. Or so help me, I'm going to murder you, and that will be the end of it."

"You do know that they record the conversations that go on between you and the visitors you might have. I've heard that you've been threatening your cellmate down the hall, too. Not very smart if you were to ask me. Not that I think you've ever been, but that's all on you." She asked her what she was talking about. "Never mind. Just get whatever you want to say to me out of your system, and I'll be on my way. The only reason that I'm going to be at your court hearing in the morning is because I want to make sure that you have a nice, long stay in some prison somewhere. That's the least that you deserve."

"I'm going to get out, and you had better pay the bail money." She told her no, she wasn't, and that pissed her off. "I wish I'd never had you. You should have been aborted like all the other brats that I got caught with."

"I figured as much. Is that the reason that Dad left you? He found out your true self? I'm betting he was disappointed in you every day. I know that I have been." She told her that she didn't care what her opinion was of her. "Obviously. You only have one thought in your head at any given time, and that's what others can do for you. Isn't that right?"

"And why shouldn't I have what I want? I'm not like those other people who work hard daily for a buck or two at the end of the week. After paying bills, there should be more to life than just working and dying. I'm going to live out a wonderful life, and you're going to do what I tell you." She said that she wasn't going to do anything for her, least of all to pay her bail. "You will, or I'll get someone to kill you. I'm not above having Carl come after you again, with the only job is to make you suffer before he kills you."

"Didn't you hear? He's dead. His bruin killed him when he was caught doing your bidding. I guess they spared him no mercy either." She told her she was a liar. "No, that would be you, and why would I care enough to tell a lie about the man that would beat me when he found me for no other reason than your bidding."

"He was a good man and a perfect henchman. If what you say about him is true and I have no reason to believe you, then I'll have to find someone else to kill you." She told her good luck with that. "Oh, don't you fret about that. I always get what I want when I want it. You're the only holdup in my perfect scheme in life. And I'll get what I want from you, too. I'm thinking millions of dollars should be enough to start my life out on a good note. Then after that, you'll make sure that I never have to do without again."

"In your dreams. I'm not going to help you do anything. Even if I could, there is no reason that you think in your small mind that I'd help you at all. But I don't know what it is you're talking about." She called her a liar again. "Whatever. I don't care what you want. I'm finished with you and your demands."

"We'll see what you're finished with when I say so." When Tabby laughed, she tried to think what it was that she said that was so funny. When she couldn't think of a single thing, she stood up close to the bars. "Come closer to me so that I can show you what it is to deny me what I want. You'll see that I'm going to get what I want when I want it, or you'll be dead. I don't even care if I have to live off of welfare for the rest of my life. You'll be dead and I'll be much happier."

"But broke according to you." She hadn't thought of that, and it pissed her off. "I'm going home now to the man that I love. You might want to think about that when you're spouting off your accusations about what I can do and not do for you. I'm in love and I've never been happier. The only thing that could make me happier is if you were sent away to prison for the rest of your life." Then she turned and walked away out of the area.

"Come back here right now, or so help me I'm going to kill you right where you stand." The laughter again had her seeing red, and she had a headache as well. "I swear to you, Tabitha Williams, I'm going to kill you as soon as I'm out of here, and I will be getting out. You just wait and see."

She heard the big door slam shut, and she grabbed the bars and screamed while shaking them. It didn't make her feel any better, but it did give her a pain right behind her eyes that hurt like hell. She wanted her daughter dead, and she wanted her to suffer. While she didn't believe that Carl was dead, she'd not been able to get in touch with him for several days now. That was when someone nudged at her mind like they were asking permission to talk.

"Who is this?" She thought for sure it was going to be Carl, and that was just one more thing she was going to be pissed off at Tabby about. Lying to her own mother was about as bad as her telling her no, she wasn't going to help her. "I said, who is this and I want you to answer me."

"It's Sirous Smith, husband to your daughter. I'm going to murder you if you upset her one more time, and I won't make it easy either." She told him she wasn't afraid of someone who would marry her daughter. *"You should be. I'm an old and very powerful vampire. I will —"*

"There is no such thing as vampires. I asked around and people said that they're a myth from some books that authors tell to sell books. I know better. What are you? Some kind of mouse or something? That would be the only type of person she could get to marry her." He said he'd come to her. *"Sure, you will, and I'm going to win the next beauty pageant that happens around here."*

A man suddenly appeared to her on the other side of the bars. He didn't look like he could shift into a mouse, but then she didn't know any mousey shifters. As he stood there, dressed from head to toe in black, she thought that he'd read the same books that she had. Where all vampires wore a custom black suit so they'd look scary. This man only looked like a young handsome man that might have been in his mid-twenties or thereabouts. He certainly didn't look like someone that she should be afraid of.

"What is it you want?" He told her. That was when she saw the fangs. "I'm not going to leave her alone. She's my daughter, and I'm going to do to her what I want. And what I want right now is for her to be dead. The sooner the better."

"It's not going to help you to have people thinking that you're talking to yourself." She asked him what he meant. "While I'm here, I'm not being recorded. Just you are. And they do record you when you're in the jail system."

"You're nuts. If I'm talking to someone, then they have to know that there is someone there. What is it you really want? I have money. Or I will have it when Tabby gets off her high horse and gets it for me. She's got her some powerful magic that tells me when the ponies are going to win their races. Can you imagine the amount of money I'm going to win when she gets around to telling me who they are? It's going to be millions." He said, not if she didn't want to help her, she wouldn't. "She'll help me, or I'll kill her. If I can't get her to do what I want, then I'm going to have her killed so that nobody can have any of the riches that she can claim for me."

"Do you ever listen to what you're saying? You sound like you have no idea what you're talking about at any given time. This is the second time I've spoken to you, and it's twice that you have made no sense." She told him to fuck off and felt good about herself for telling him that when he looked so shocked. "Great comeback. I'm sure you threaten everyone that way. It's not going to do you any good to get out of jail, which you're not, because I'll be watching you."

She felt a breeze of air around her body, and she swayed slightly. The pain in her throat had her putting her hand there, and it came away with blood. Just a little bit, but it was enough to have her thinking she might have been wrong about what he was. Linda looked to where he'd been standing and asked where he'd gone.

"I'm here." He was sitting on her cot now, and he looked bigger than he had standing in the hallway. "You should really believe me when I tell you what I am. I have a taste of you now, so I'll be able to know what you're thinking all the time. Also, where you are. You'll never be able to hide from me."

"Like I care." Slightly dizzy, she went to the wall furthest away from her cot and leaned against it. She wasn't going to let him know that she felt off, but she did have to hold onto it so that she'd not fall on her ass. "I'm no more afraid of you than I am of my daughter. She's a whimp just like you and your little mousey friends are."

He stood up then, and she could see that he was much larger than she'd first thought, like several feet taller than she was at just under six feet. When he put out his hands, they elongated into fingers that stretched out several inches beyond the fingertips. Then she looked at his face.

His boyish charm was gone, and in its place was a face that nightmares were made of. His eyes were the color of blood, and his fangs were now the length of her smallest finger and extra sharp. Backing up more against the wall, she turned her head and closed her eyes when he took two steps toward her. Christ, he was a monster.

"I am a monster and you'll never forget that." He ran a finger down her cheek, and she whimpered softly. Fear like she'd never felt had her toes curl up and her fingers clinch. "I will not allow you to treat my mate the way that you have. Do you understand me? You'll leave her alone, or so help me, I'll kill you so that there isn't enough of you to look for when I finish. Have I made myself clear to you?"

"Yes. You're not right in the head." He laughed, and even it sounded scary to her ears. "Leave me alone before I call the police on you. They'll come running too when I yell for them."

"You can try that, but they'll never see me." He was standing on the other side of the bars just as normal as he'd been before. "I'm leaving you now, Linda Ann Williams. You remember that I know all there is to know about you, and you might just live a bit longer. Doubtful that you'll heed my words, but I've said all I'm saying to you before I come after you again. I will strike, and you'll be dead. I promise you."

He was gone after that. She stood where she'd been standing for a long time, fearful that he'd be back. When one of the officers came to bring her the meal that she'd ordered yesterday, she told him about the man. He told her to behave herself and not try to get out of going to the courthouse tomorrow. That was when it occurred to her to expose him too. Vampires were real, and she knew just where one was living.

"Stupid old fool. He just gave me what I wanted without me having to threaten him." Laughing out loud, she even enjoyed her meal of a hamburger and fries. The meat was just a little underdone, but she found that she liked it. Yes, she was going to expose the idiot, and that would mean a great deal more money for her when it came out. "People will want to know my story, and I'll give it to them for a price."

When she went to bed that night, she was actually happy. It wouldn't be long now before she'd be in the courthouse telling it all. He'd made a mistake, and she was going to profit from it. And they'd let her go because she was special enough for a vampire to have exposed himself to her, too. Linda was going to be a millionaire, and she'd not have to work all that hard at becoming one, either.

~*~

Sirous liked it when a plan came together. He knew what Linda was going to try to do tomorrow, but it would backfire on her. Everyone in town knew that they were vampires, but kept it to themselves because of the help they did for the town. Money had a way of keeping the best-kept secrets quiet, and he was hoping that was true for him as well. He told Brew what his plan had been before he left.

"They really couldn't care less until something happens." He asked him what that would be. "People turning up dead for no reason. Drained bodies hanging in the rafters. I know we don't do things like that, but so long as it's not happening, they don't mind keeping our secrets. And so long as when they need something, we're willing to pay more than our fair share of it to be fixed or replaced."

"Like the schools?" He said that was only a small part of what they did for the town. "I noticed that several projects are going on at once around here. Like the renovation of the courthouse. Is that something that you're involved in?"

"Only slightly. But yes, we have a hand in just about anything that goes on around here. I like it that way too. They don't tell the newspapers what we are, and we can live in relative quiet while the town does well." Sirous asked if he was upset that the woman would be exposing them. "No. She's only one person who thinks that she saw something while under arrest in our jails. I love the fact that you made it so that you weren't recorded. She'll just look like a fool talking to herself. I love that plan."

"Thanks. I wish I could take credit, but it was Kenneth who gave me the idea. He said that he used it once when he'd been being blackmailed by someone, and it had worked. The man was shipped off to the loony bin, and everyone made out well because he put in all the new sidewalks in the town. He said it cost him very little in the long run and was happy with the results." Brew asked him if he'd been blackmailed by the priest. "He didn't say. Maybe that's it. But like I said, he didn't give me those details. You'll have to tell me about that sometime. Or I'll ask him. It sounds like a good story."

"It is. It's an old one, but a good one too. The priest had been doing some underhanded things with the church money, and he wanted Kenneth to pay it all back. As you can imagine, it's much longer than that, but you get the idea. Ask him about it. It's a good story to hear." Sirous said that he would and soon. "We are all planning to go to the courthouse in the morning. In support of the two of you. It might be funny to hear her going on about a vampire when there will be six in the room with her. I do wonder sometimes if humans knew about us for sure, if they'd be so generous with their time. I have some good friends who are humans now, and I'd hate to lose them because of some woman."

"You won't. She'll make her statements, and that will be the end of it after she's laughed off the dais. She's been spreading it around that Tabitha can tell which races the horses are going to win. This will just be one more thing to have her looked at oddly when she's around people. Did I tell you that she can read the lottery numbers as well? Her mother doesn't know that. I can't wait until tomorrow to see how things go." He said they were all looking forward to it. "Good. I know that Tabitha and I are going to enjoy her going to jail again."

"Do you think that she will? I mean, what has she done wrong but threatened Tabby? There is no law that will get her prison time for that, I don't think." He said that she had hired Carl to kill her daughter. "Yes, that's her word against Linda's. I don't know, Sirous. She might be out before we can see a reason for that not to happen. That would be bad for her, no doubt, but it would still have her out there going after the two of you again."

"I guess we'll have to wait and see. I never thought that she'd be getting out for threatening her own daughter with death. I mean, if one of us were threatened, they'd be dead before they could get within a mile of us. That's just the way things would go. But this is something that the humans will decide." He looked at his old friend. "Do you really think she'll be getting out? That would upset Tabitha a great deal. I can protect her to a point, but she'd still be out there all the time."

"You couldn't kill her either. Not with her threatening you with exposure. That would bring people looking into her death." He said he'd not thought of that either. "We'll have to think of something to keep Tabby safe. Even if we have to send her away when she tries to expose us. She'll still be a threat to Tabby."

"I'll give it some thought. I don't suppose that you got with the burin about her making Carl do the things that he'd done." Brew told him that the burin was satisfied with the way things had ended for the man, and they wanted nothing to do with a human. "I don't blame them there. Not at all."

For the rest of the evening, he tried to think of ways to get Linda out of their lives. And Brew had been right. They couldn't just kill her because that would bring people out of the woodwork, trying to figure out what had happened to her. She wasn't anyone important in anyone's lives, but she had a name for herself when it came to this little town. Yes, even though killing her would solve a lot of problems, it would just make more for them if they were to do it.

Sirous told Tabitha what was going on. She didn't seem worried about her mother getting out, and he couldn't blame her for that. It was her mother after all. And while she didn't like her overly much, she was still the person who gave birth to her. At least that's what he figured. He wanted to comfort her about her, but she seemed resolved in the opinion that her mother wasn't getting out of jail. And she didn't have a reason either. She just believed it.

"I've decided that I'm going to wear a different colored suit to the courthouse tomorrow." Tabitha just stared at him. "I was thinking blue or brown, but nothing too bright. It occurred to me that I've been wearing the same color suit since I was changed. It was the thing to do back then, to dress in black because we had money. I've noticed that Brew has been wearing jeans and t-shirts a bit more, too. What do you say?"

"I'd ask you what made you decide? I've been complaining about you wearing all black for a while now." He said that her mother had pointed it out that he was dressed in black from head to toe. "Yes, you have been. And I know you want to wear a suit tomorrow, but how about if you wear a pair of shorts for—no, not shorts. I believe that your legs would be so white that it would be blinding."

"Oh my, was that a shot at my being a vampire?" He tickled her then and had her laughing hard. "I do believe that you've teased yourself into a corner. I will show off my blinding white legs tomorrow just so you can be embarrassed about them. What do you think of that?"

"I think that if that doesn't proclaim you as a vamp, then nothing will. But you really should wear some jeans and some comfy shirts. Wearing a tie all the time has to be too much. Have you ever worn anything but suits?" He told her that when he'd been younger, but they weren't black suits, but more colorful at one time. "I can't imagine you in anything but what you're wearing now. Change into something like I said and let me see you."

He willed jeans and a sweatshirt on. It was comfortable, but it felt like he was wearing someone else's clothing. Sirous looked into her eyes and was shocked to see humor there. He asked her what was so funny. It took her twenty minutes to stop laughing so she could tell him that he did look like a different person in them.

"This was your idea. What on earth could be that funny?" She would look at him and burst out laughing again. It wasn't that he was hurt by her laughing at him; he had hoped to put her in a better mood, but he was surprised that she thought him to look so funny in something that she wore every day. "Tell me what has you busting up like you are."

"I just never thought of you in jeans and a sweatshirt, I guess. I thought that when you stopped wearing suits, it would still be dress pants and a nice polo shirt. Not that you don't look good in what you have on, it's just not what I expected. I love it. And you." He had a feeling that it was more than that, but didn't try to get more out of her. "You need some tennis shoes now. Dress shoes are nice with jeans, but only if you're going out or something."

For the rest of the afternoon, he changed clothing to suit her. She wasn't laughing any longer, but she was helping him find a style. While he did like wearing jeans when they were together, he was happier with the dress pants and a nice button-down shirt. He could even wear a tie with it if he wanted to dress up. By the time they had exhausted all sorts of styles of clothing for him, he'd picked out one that suited him best. He loved to be clean-looking and dressed up a bit, too. He did wonder what the others would think of his new mode of dress and decided that he didn't care. Tabitha was happy, and that was all that he cared about right now.

When they made their way up to bed, having dinner out on the deck had been nice, and the two of them got into bed and held each other. They'd made love before dinner, and she was tired, so he only held her tonight so that she could rest. He'd not mentioned that she'd been having bad dreams, and when she had one, he'd put her into a deeper sleep, but he was worried about her all the same because of her mother. Something was going to happen tomorrow, and he had a feeling that it was going to be bad for his little family. Sirous would go to jail for his mate if it came to that, and he would gladly take any blame, too, if she were to do something to her mother.

He hoped that it wouldn't come to that, but he just didn't know. Rolling to his back, taking Tabitha with him, he held her tightly while she slept. Tomorrow was going to be good or bad, and there wasn't going to be any gray area either. It would be all good, or it would end badly. Any way he saw it happening wasn't good, and that scared him more than just a little bit.

As the sun was coming up, he checked in on Linda. She was resolved to expose him, and he thought it funny. There were thoughts about her daughter in her mind and exposing her as well, but mostly she was centered on having him get into trouble. What sort of trouble he didn't understand in her mind, but it was there for him to see that she wanted him dead and out of her daughter's life. So that she'd do what she wanted. That wasn't going to happen either, as Tabitha had turned into a very strong-willed person and wouldn't be bullied by her mother again.

Chapter 9

The courtroom was packed, and she thought it was all for her mother. When the judge said he was going to hear several cases today, he also told them that he wanted no shenanigans either. He wanted things to be orderly and quiet so that he could get out of here at a good time. She didn't see how that was going to happen when there was so much noise in the room, now you could barely hear him talking. But she didn't know what was going to happen today, so she let him rule the room. Her mother was fifth in line to be seen, and she was glad she'd gotten there early to be able to see her in action.

The first judgment didn't go as planned. Even she could see that. The man who had been brought from the jailhouse decided that he didn't want his day in court today, as his wife and children weren't present. The judge, Judge Jim Markus, said he didn't care about his family and told them to go forward. He wanted his family there to say he'd been a good man, but had slipped up when he'd gotten drunk and beat the shit out of his wife and two of his kids. He was remanded over to a jury trial, and he'd spend his time in jail waiting for a date that could be agreed upon. Of course, that didn't go over very well, and it took a good half hour to get everyone to settle down again.

"I'm going to be an easy trial, your excellency. I just want out of jail so that I can spend some time with my daughter and her new husband." Her mother had stood up when the room was getting settled down. "I don't have any drunken things on my docket, nor do I want any special treatment. I just want to be released. I think I've been a model captive, and I want out now."

"We have an order to things and I won't have you messing things up for me." He picked up a file, and before he could read whatever was on it, her mother appealed again to be released. "Everyone in here wants to be released. I'm not in the mood to just give a sweeping release of people just because they have a daughter who just got married. Sit down and shut up until I call your name."

"It's Linda Williams. I'm sure that you have it right there in front of you. If not, the man behind you who's hovering can find it for you." Mother paused and smiled. "I just found out that my daughter is married to a vampire and that she can tell me who's going to win the races at the racetrack."

The room went silent. Even the bailiff behind the judge stopped in mid-sentence to whatever he was saying to the judge. Everyone turned and looked at her mother, and she just kept staring at the judge and smiling. He asked her what she'd said.

"My daughter. She has this special magic that allows her to see when the ponies come in to win, and I've won a lot of money from her. Her husband, that man over there beside her, is a vampire. I saw him with his fangs. He came to see me in jail just last night." Everyone turned to look where she was pointing, and she stood up. There wasn't any way that she was going to be blackmailed into doing what her mother wanted now that she'd exposed her to everyone. "See her? She's not too terribly pretty, but she does have that magic. I'm assuming that's why the vampire married her, so that he could have the money that belongs to me. She owes me for me bringing her into this world. If not, then I'm going to kill her and that husband of hers. Just why he's out in the sunlight now is a mystery to me, but he said he was old."

"You want us to believe that your daughter is married to a vampire? And that she has magic, too, that knows the winning horse when there are races?" Mother nodded and said that what she was saying was true. "I see. You really believe this. There is no such thing as magic, and there certainly isn't anything like vampires around. Unless you mean an attorney. I was one once, so I know what I'm talking about." He laughed a little, and it fell on deaf ears. "I don't know what you're playing at, but I won't have my courtroom disrupted because you have a burr up your bottom. And I won't have you threatening anyone while I'm up on this seat. You'll sit down and be quiet, or so help me I'll send you back to jail where you'll stay."

"I know for a fact that he's a vampire. He told me so. You have to record the things that go on in a jail cell, so have them bring it up and tell them to read it to you. Or you could put it on one of those big-screen televisions. I don't care. I just know what he told me." She looked at her then. "See? I will get what I want, and you're going to suffer from it. I don't care if the whole world knows what you can do and wants some of it from you. I'm going to get what I want, or I'll kill you. It's as simple as that."

"Nothing is as simple as that." Judge Markus banged his gavel down on the small wooden board and said he wanted order in his room. She thought that the room was waiting for something else to flow from her mother's mouth that would qualify her to be sent away. "I'm not through with you yet, and you'll sit down and shut up. Think very hard about what you're saying, Ms. Williams, or you'll be sent back to jail, where you'll hear about your judgment later. I told you that I wanted nothing like this to happen in my courtroom today, and I demand that you sit down and shut your trap."

Mother finally sat down, but she had the strangest smile on her face. It would have scared her a little had she not known that her mother was going to be tried for being insane. Who went around spouting about vampires and magic when they had no proof at all of it? She was going to end up in the loony bin if it was the last thing that she did.

The next three verdicts went without incident. They were given a fine to pay and time served on their judgment. The fourth one was a little more complicated in that several witnesses testified that he'd been doing whatever he'd been doing when he'd been arrested. She had tuned them out and was thinking about her mother.

Tabby had never realized just how selfish her mother was until recently. She knew that she wanted things that were out of her reach all the time, but she never put it to anything but her having nothing as a child. But then she'd never known any of her grandparents, and for all she knew, they'd given her everything that she wanted and more.

What little she knew of her mother's childhood was more than likely lies that she'd made up to make herself the victim. And she was good at making herself out to be that. Everything was about her, and if it wasn't, she'd make it so that it was just to get the attention that she supposed she deserved.

When her mother's name was said, she turned to look at the judge. He wasn't happy, it seemed, and she couldn't begin to fathom why. Something must have happened, like her mother had set him off again. She hoped that he would throw the book at her for her sentencing, and she'd be thrilled beyond words to have her out of her hair.

"It says here that you were only visited by your daughter yesterday, yet you claim that a vampire, Mr. Smith, came to visit you and told you that he was a vampire. Is that what you're telling me?" She said that he wasn't able to be recorded because of what he was. "I see. He told you this, did he?"

"No. He didn't have to. I've read enough books about his kind to know that they can't see their reflections, nor can they be recorded. Also, they're afraid of garlic." He asked why they were afraid of garlic. "I don't know, that's just what the books said."

"More than one is there. Tell me, what's the name of the book so that I can see for myself what it says." She told him two books, and they both sounded like romance books. Apparently, the judge thought so as well. "Are those romance books? Books of fiction, I might add."

"Everyone knows that they have an insider view on the shifters of the world. There are those as well. I've hired one to kill my daughter. Well, he was supposed to bring her to me, but all he managed to do was get himself killed. He was a bear shifter, and I heard that his bruin had him killed for his help in helping me bring my daughter to me." He just stared at her. If she didn't know for a fact that she was telling the truth, Tabby might well think she was nuts as well. "It's all in the books that I was telling you about. All you need to do is pick up one with a handsome guy on the front of the cover, and you'll get all the information you need about them. Especially vampires. That's all they seem to want to write about. I personally think that all shifters are sexier than a vampire. All those sharp teeth and all."

"I don't care what you think is sexier, Ms. Williams. We're here to determine if you're fit enough to stand trial. It started out with you being in jail for threatening your daughter, but I think we've gone well beyond that, don't you think?" She asked him if he was making fun of her. "I do believe that I am. No one but you seems to believe that there are shifters in the world, much less vampires that are afraid of garlic. You never did answer me about why they're afraid of the thing either."

"I said I don't know, but that's what I read." He nodded as if that explained it. "Ask him what he is if you don't believe me. And ask my daughter about having the insider information about the horse races that are going on."

"Mr. Smith, I hate to ask this, but are you a vampire?" He said not only was he not one, but he didn't believe in them either. "I didn't think so. Mrs. Smith, do you have insider information on the horse races? You don't really have to answer that. I don't believe you would be able to predict the outcome of races anyway. This is just a formality, you understand."

"No, sir. I can't tell the outcome of the races. If I had, I'd be on some tropical island right now instead of here with my mother spouting off things that come from a romance novel that someone has written." She asked for permission to speak to him. When it was given, she nodded once to make sure that he understood how upset she was. "Is she going to be able to get out to roam free, sir? I mean, she's threatened to kill me no less than five times since yesterday. And even when she was behind bars, she made it clear that I wasn't going to be around much longer. What's going to happen when she gets out and is free to roam the streets? Streets that I walk on daily? Am I going to have to hire myself a bodyguard to keep me safe from my own mother?"

"She's lying." The judge asked her mother what she had been lying about. "Every word out of her mouth is a lie. I did threaten to kill her, but who wouldn't if she didn't help them get enough money to live off of? Anyone would. But she's being selfish. And she can too tell you what the horse races are. Just ask her to give them to you."

"Ms. Williams, I've had about enough of your telling me what to do in my own courtroom." She told him that he should do things right. "In your favor, no doubt. I won't do that, and I take threatening people very seriously. You'll be remanded over for a trial and stay in jail while you await things to be set up. Also, I want you to be tested for your competence to stand trial. I think that something is wrong with you."

"The only thing that is wrong with me is that my daughter isn't giving me what I want. Damn it all to fuck and back, what the hell is wrong with you? I've told you what they are. Isn't there some law about people lying about what they are? If not, then there should be. He's a fucking vampire, and she's got magic too. And if they've slept together, there is no telling how much more magic she has. The same books say that about them, too." He asked her if she meant the romance novels. "Of course, that's what I'm talking about. Where else is a person supposed to get their information than that? She's probably a fucking vampire by now, too. You know that the blood is better for them if she's coming when he drinks from her."

"I've heard quite enough." When he banged his gavel again, he ordered her mother to be taken back to jail and her to stay there. "You've messed with the wrong man in this courtroom today, and I want it to be known that you're off your noodle."

"I want her to give me what I want. Are you listening to me? She's got magic, and I want a part of it so that I can be rich. Are you listening to me?" She was dragged away, screaming about blood and magic. Tabby sat down in her chair and looked at Sirous. He looked like he was on the verge of losing it when she asked him what was wrong.

"Nothing. Not really. However, I think it's funny when I know for a fact that the judge is a leopard shifter that has quite a large claw of cats around here." She looked at the judge who was calling the next case. It was almost too funny for her, and she needed to get out of here before she lost it. He stood right there at the front of the courtroom and asked about shifters and romance books like he wasn't one of the ones mentioned in them.

She was barely out the door when she started laughing. It was something that she thought that she could laugh about for the rest of her life, the look on the judge's face when her mother was talking about shifters as if he wasn't one himself. Yes, she thought, she'd be laughing about that for the next hundred or so years.

~*~

Sirous thought it was wonderful how much he laughed nowadays. He'd been in such a funk for the last thousand years or so that he found himself sore from laughing so much. He supposed that being in love helped a great deal as well.

And he was in love with Tabitha. Daily, she made him happy that Yosef hadn't killed him. Even when he'd begged him to, he'd not done it because he'd found his mate. Sirous had given him the pick of the treasures from the paintings and sculptures, but he felt like he needed to do more for him. He owed him, quite literally, his life, and he thought he'd be a long time in paying him back for it too.

"Have you ever given information to a writer about your kind? It seems to me that they had a great deal of it wrong but enough right to make it believable." He said that he'd never done it, no, but he did know of vamps that had. Just enough to make them believe them. "I see. Well, it's kind of scary the information they have, I think. I'm betting that the one about reflections and garlic has gotten you out of a sticky situation."

"Yes. Then, when you reach a certain age, it's nice to be able to see the sun rise. That one has saved me more than the garlic test. I have learned to eat a whole clove of it without even a grimace. Nasty stuff, but I can do it." She laughed, and he had to admire once again how beautiful she was. "I've not told you because when I'm around you, I nearly forget my name, but we are legally married in the eyes of the law. It was filed some weeks back when we got together. That way, there's no question when you were able to use my credit cards."

"Good. I don't need a ceremony anyway. I'm just happy that we're together." He said that he was as well and kissed her on the nose. "What do we do now? I mean, besides living our lives the way that we want them. I've no doubt that my mother is going to be found not fit to stand trial and be sent away. I hope so anyway. It's nice not to have to worry about her trying to kill me at every turn."

"I know you understand this, but there is no way she would have been able to kill you. I wanted you to understand that she'd have to remove your head the same as she would me. It's not going to happen. Not that I can see her trying to do that, but you can be hurt. Not badly, but something like a broken bone will heal quickly, but it'll hurt all the same." She asked if he'd broken anything of late. "Nothing that I can worry enough over. I've been hurt before. Someone will get it in their head to shoot someone, and I'll be standing there, but nothing that I'd not heal from. Not even silver will bother me at this stage of my life. The only thing that could harm you is childbirth. Again, it's only pain and nothing that will kill you."

"Will we have children?" Sirous told her that it would be totally up to her, as it was her body. "That doesn't tell me if you want to have children or not. Do you want some little ones running around? I know that Calla is breeding, I think you call it, and Brew seems to be happy about it. So do you want children with me or not?"

"I do. As many as you want, I'll be there for you and them." He put his hand on her flat belly and smiled. "You're not breeding now, but you could be if we keep making love daily like we are. I can tell when you're ovulating and when you're with child, but that's about all I know. I believe that Brew could tell us more, but I'd just as soon not have him having more information than we do about our child."

"Do you think we could wait a while? I feel like I've just been given my freedom from my mother and would like to enjoy getting to know you better." He said that she would wait as long as she wanted, and that he wanted to get to know her better as well. "We have so much time to have children that I find myself thinking about all the things I want to do with you while we still are just the two of us."

"I understand. It seems like we learn more about each other daily, and I love that. I know things about you that I'm sure not even your mother would know." She didn't doubt that; she told him because he listened to her. "I do. I hang on every word you say to me because I love you. Very much, my dear."

When she sat across his lap, he held her to him. She rode his cock for several minutes until he willed his pants off. As soon as she was as naked as he was, he lifted her up so that she could ride him with her pussy. Sirous suckled at her breasts as she held onto his shoulders. He enjoyed this time with her, making love whenever it suited them. She was right in that a child right now would change things for them, and he did wonder if they'd ever not want each other with as much passion as he did right now. He certainly hoped not. He loved making love to her all over the house.

"You're so hard when I do this." He said that he was forever hard when she was around. "Surely not all the time. How would you think with all your blood rushing to your cock all the time?" She sighed heavily as she leaned up closer to his mouth. "I want to bite you. Do you think that would be possible?"

He nearly came; he was so excited about her question. "I don't see any reason why not. Even if you were to take my blood into your body, it would make me come so hard that I'd probably test my immortality a bit."

Sirous rolled her to her back and settled between her legs. She held him tightly between her legs, and he made love to her slowly. It was times like this that he was glad for a large couch. It was great to snuggle on, but better to make love on too.

Kissing her brought him so much pleasure. The darkness of her mouth was sweet and warm. He enjoyed tangling with her tongue and nipping at it with his teeth. When she moaned that she was coming, he watched her face as she stiffened beneath him and came. He would never get enough of that and made love to her again while her body adjusted to his. Christ, he loved this woman.

Stretching her arms above her head, he ran his fingers back down them and watched her shudder. Her muscles quivered a bit, and he wanted to have her wrapped around him. But he wanted her to be in a position to bite him if she could. If nothing else, he could make a cut along his heart and have her drink from him there. Whatever she wanted, he did as well.

Suckling at her breasts, he loved the sounds she made when she was enjoying herself. The small moans and a little bit of hissing breath took his breath away. He could tell when she would come; her body responded so well to his that they were in tune with one another. Sirous could wait forever to come so long as she was enjoying herself when they had sex. And they certainly did love to have sex. All over the house, it seemed to him.

"My body aches for something only you can give me." He asked her what that was. "I don't know. But I have a feeling that it's right there on the tip of my tongue. Have you been holding back on me?"

"Never." He kissed her deeply and smiled down at her as he moved his cock deep inside of her and out again. "I'd give you my all if you wanted it. Everything that I have is yours forever, my love."

They made love slowly. Each of them giving and taking what was there for them. Sirous loved the taste of her skin, the silky smoothness of it. The way her dark hair spread out beneath the two of them. It too was silky, and he thought that when she wore it down, it was the sexiest thing he'd ever seen.

"I need to come." He nodded and told her that he wanted her to bite him. "Oh yes, that's what I want to. I feel the need to drink from you, too. Would that be all right?"

"Yes." He felt his cock move deeper inside of her at the thought of her at his throat. He would do whatever she wanted, but he surely hoped that she could bite him. As he leaned down to her mouth, his cock moving in and out of her quicker, he felt her tongue taste his throat before she sank her teeth into his neck.

"Christ." He came hard inside of her, pounding her pretty pussy as he emptied himself deep inside of her. When she drew in some of his blood, he nearly passed out with the pleasure of it and was ready to come again. When she cried out around his throat that she was coming too, it was all he could do not to throw back his head and howl. He'd never in his life had wanted to do that at any time of his life. "Come for me. Come now."

She came again and again as she drank from him. When her small tongue sealed the wounds at his throat, he pounded her hard until he could almost feel her moving away from him as he slid her up on the couch. As soon as he came this time, he knew that he was going to pass out and held tightly onto Tabitha so that she would not get away from him.

When he woke up, he was still on the couch but alone now. He wanted to get up and find Tabitha, but he was just too relaxed to move. Reaching out beyond the room he was in, he found her in their bathroom taking a shower. Oh, to have that much energy when he'd just made love to the most wonderful creature in the world. Sitting up, he looked around the room.

They'd made a mess of the couch. He'd have to allow the sunlight in to take care of the blood stains on it, but wasn't overly worried. If it came to that, he'd just buy another couch and be done with the one that they'd ruined. Standing up, he had to sit down quickly as his head was spinning. Sitting on the couch for a few minutes more, he realized that he was stronger, too. Like he'd fed recently and had fed well. He wondered how Tabitha felt now that she'd drunk from him and decided to go up and find out.

"I was just coming to wake you. I needed a shower. I was covered in blood." He told her that he thought that they'd ruined the couch. "We didn't ruin it, we broke it in. I loved every moment of it, too." They both laughed, and he felt better for taking her so hard.

"There are some things that I'd like to talk to you about. Did you know that when you bit me, you had fangs? It could be because you have a little bit of vampire in your lineage." She said that she didn't know that, but was glad that it could make it more enjoyable for the two of them. "Both of the vampires are dead now. They met the sun when their mates died. It's sad when that happens."

"I don't know what I'd do without you with me. I know that I'd want to die as well. You can't leave me, Sirous. Ever. I can't live without you in my life." He said that he felt the same way about her. "Good, then we have a deal. We will live forever and not leave the other behind."

They talked about her vampire blood for a bit more before Tabitha told him that she was hungry. As they made their way down to the kitchen after he had a shower as well, she was happy to find a platter of sandwiches in the refrigerator. Their new cook was working out better than he ever dreamed that she would, and he was glad that she was forever thinking about leaving snacks like the sandwiches for Tabitha to have. She was hungry all the time now, and he knew that it had to do with them making love so much. They burned a great deal of calories when they had sex, and he couldn't have been happier.

"We should have the others over for talking. I know that you and Calla will want food, but the rest of us can talk about when we were younger. There are some stories that I think you'd enjoy." She said that sounded wonderful. "It's not like we can have a dinner party or anything, but we can enjoy the company of our friends. I'm afraid that we spend too much time just hanging around the house. We need to get out more."

"I understand what you're saying, but I so love just spending time with you. How about we have them over tomorrow night? That'll give us plenty of time to change out the couch for a newer one. I'm afraid for them to speculate on what happened to it." He told her that they'd all know, as they were vampires as well. "I suppose I'll have to get used to that. Them knowing everything that we do. It's a vampire thing, I suppose."

"It's more of a male thing, I believe." She smacked him on the arm, and he kissed her. They were such a good couple that he worried at times when something was going to happen. He'd never been one to think that the other shoe was going to drop, but of late, that's all he could think about. He didn't want to have anything happen to either of them, but he was sure something was about to come along and test them.

Chapter 10

It didn't take as long as he thought to get the building up and under construction. There was a lot to be said for magic in abundance, and Rance had a great deal of it. Getting the water lines hooked up to the bathrooms in the building was easier than he thought it would be, so he finished those up in no time. His house was going to be a showcase when he was finished with it, and one that he thought he could live in for the rest of his life. He only hoped that if a mate came along, she was under the same assumption as he was that going green was better than using up all the resources in the little town that he lived in.

Petunia, his faerie, came to sit on his hand. It was somewhat startling to him when she did that, but he had not had the heart to tell her that she couldn't do that. He just smiled at her when she asked if she could tell him something.

"Of course you can. At any time." She fluttered her tiny wings and rose up from his hand several inches before she settled back down. "What is it you have to tell me?"

"There is a man in town who is looking to buy

up land. He has it in his head that the land you bought belongs to him. I've checked the records, and you've been the owner for quite some time now, and there is no record of him owning anything around here." He asked her for his name. "Walter Hudson. There are other records about him with the police department, but they're not anything that would make me believe that he's here on good terms. I believe that he is scamping people."

He corrected her. "Scamming people is something that happens all the time. I'd like to say that it's just humans that do it, but all shifters and vampires do the same. Especially when there is something that they want." She told him that it was sad. "It is at that. But this man, what do you know of him other than he thinks that the land I've owned for decades is his? I'm sure you've been following him around to get as much information about him as you can."

"I have. He is staying at the hotel that is in Columbus and drives here daily to look at the public records that are filed downtown. I think he's looking for land to take over all over. He's been writing down the names of people that I believe he hopes to scam out of their land." He asked her if she had a list of the names as well, and should have known that she would. "I have them marked off, too, when he goes and visits them. He is pushy for a human, but then I think that all humans are pushy to a point. I don't know that I care much for them. Pushy people, I mean."

"I don't either, to be honest. They usually get their comeuppance once things start to fall apart around them." She agreed with him, but he had a feeling that she didn't understand what he was talking about. "Keep an eye on him so that we can know his next move. My home should be finished in a couple more days, and then I'm going to start moving in the things that I've already purchased for it."

"Very good, sir." When she left him, he got back to work on the water lines. There were things that he wanted to incorporate in his house that he knew were going to save water as well as electricity. He had been studying up on things for a long time and knew just what he wanted in the way of his home.

It was so easy for him to do the work that he wanted that he would often find his mind drifting. And of late, it had been about finding a mate. Not that he didn't want one, but he didn't want her to be human. Being around the other two women showed him that they were a great deal of work, and they were just too young for him.

He often thought himself too set in his ways for a mate. He liked to do things on his own time and didn't want to have to wait on someone else when it was time for him to go. He'd not see that in the other two mates, but he was sure he was going to get a dud when it came to mates. She'd be forever making him late for things, and that wouldn't sit well with him.

Also, there was the age difference. He was simply too old for someone who was born at the end of his life. Not to say that he was planning on dying anytime soon, but to have a mate that would be forever wanting to have things going her way wasn't anything that he wanted. He had his life just the way that he wanted it, and be damned if he was going to change himself to suit a young upstart.

He nearly missed an entire floor of his home with the water lines as he was getting angry about the upstart. He couldn't call her that around the others. Calla would have his head, and Tabby would knock him around, too. They were upstarts as well, he thought, but he'd never say that to them. He liked his head just where it was right now.

As he finished putting in the water lines, he noticed that the front door to his home was open. He'd put up the shell of his home several weeks ago to keep others from seeing what he was doing to his home, but seeing the door open gave him a start. He made his way there now and was sure that the man who had been asking around town about his house and land was standing in the middle of his living room. He asked him what he was doing.

"The door was open, so I thought I'd see what was going on. I have just been to the courthouse, and it says that you're building on my land." Well, that was news to him, and he told him so. "Yes, well, I love the house, but I'm afraid that I'm going to have to have you stop now, as I didn't want a house put on my land. You're just lucky that I'm not going to sue you."

"Where is your proof that you own this land? I'm sure you've brought proof." He said that he hadn't brought it with him, he'd not known that someone was building on his land. "No one is building on your land, as I've owned this property for a good long time. I have a copy of the purchase agreement as well as I've been paying the land tax on it for decades."

"You don't look old enough to have owned anything for decades." He didn't bother answering the man as he knew to the day how long he'd own the property. It was well before this man had ever been born. "I do own this land, and I'm going to have to ask you to stop building. I have plans for this property, and it doesn't involve having a house sitting in the middle of the land."

"Whatever floats your boat. When you have proof that it belongs to you, you come back with the police, and we'll see who owns what. In the meantime, I'm only going to tell you this one time to get off my land and don't come back. I don't care for trespassers, and that's what you're doing." He told him that he couldn't trespass on his own land. "As I said, you come back with proof and we'll talk about it. In the meantime, I've asked you to leave, and you'd better be on your way. I'm finished talking about this."

"You're not very nice, are you. All right, I don't have proof that I own this land, but I can buy it from you twice what you paid for it. That's more than fair." He told him no. "Just like that? You're not even going to listen to the deal that I have for you? That seems like a man who doesn't have any idea what he has is worth."

"I know what it's worth as I'm building my home on it. I've no time for you, as I have said to you several times now. Move on, or I'm calling the police. You've been warned." When the man didn't move, he pulled out his cell phone to call the police. The man actually knocked the phone from his hand. Rance could feel his other half take hold of him, and he was barely able to hold him back. It would be just like this man, a human again, to try and say that he'd hurt him in some way so that the police would need to arrest him. Not today, he thought. He had better things to do other than mess with someone who didn't seem to understand that he'd said no.

Picking up his phone, he had the police dialed before he put it to his ear. Telling them that he had a problem on his land had them asking if it was Walter Hudson. Since they knew who he was, Rance figured that they'd had problems with him before. It wasn't going to bode well for the man if he kept this up. They said they were on their way.

After putting his phone away, he stared at the man. He was older than he looked, and Rance could tell that he was also sickly. There was something wrong with him, and he wondered if he knew it. Not that it mattered to him. Hudson was going to get his ass killed if he kept up doing what he was doing. And Rance really wanted to be the one who did it to him. As the police pulled into his property, he felt a little better about shoving the man off.

"Mr. Hudson, you've been warned about trespassing on other people's property twice now. This is going to get you run in if you keep harassing the good people of this town." He said that Rance had threatened him. "Of course he did. Like Mrs. Warner did when you were harassing her about her land. She's a ninety-year-old woman who has lived in that same land for the last fifty years or so. Move along, or I'm going to run you in. And you won't like that one bit when I call your boss."

"What boss?" He told him the name of the person that he worked for. "You can't do that. I'm here on sick leave. It's none of her business what I'm doing around here."

"It is if she thinks that you're sick when all you're doing is making people sick of you. Now run along. Or better yet, get back in your car and leave our town. We've got enough going on without you causing more trouble around here. I will arrest you if I have to come back out to someone's home and talk to you again." He said he was just trying to buy up land. "Oh, so now you're buying it up, are you? Last I heard, you were going to evict people like Mrs. Warner because you said you owned the land. Did they get too smart for you and turn you down? Sounds to me like you've worn out your welcome around here. Move on before I have to move you on, sir. I've had about enough of you."

"I don't understand what the issue is with people around here. My money is just as good as theirs is. Why can't I do a little negotiating while I'm in town?" He said because he was going about things all wrong. "I'm just a man who sees something here and will do what's necessary to get it taken care of. There is prime land around here, and I mean to have most of it."

"Not if people don't want to sell, you won't." The police were finally able to get the man to get moving and then asked if he wanted to press charges. All he'd done was knock his phone out of his hand

and had entered his house. For now, he was satisfied that the man was gone. "But if he returns, then all bets are off, and I'm going to not just press charges against him but make sure he understands the meaning of the word no. He doesn't seem to get that."

"I've been keeping an eye on him for the last several days. I'll do better now that he's come out here. The man isn't going to go away easily, I don't think. He has it in his head that he will own the property that he wants and damn what anyone else has to say about it. Yesterday, Mrs. Warner beat him out of her house with her broom. Did my heart good to see her taking care of business like that. She's old, but she's feisty." Rance remembered her when she was just a little girl, when he'd come to visit Brew. She'd been a handful then. "I'll be on my way, Rance. If he comes back, try not to kill him. The amount of paperwork would take me most of the day to fill out, and I want to get off early tonight to see my kids playing ball at the new field."

"You have fun. But I'm not going to be making any promises." After he left him, Rance had to shake himself several times before he could shed his anger. The man needed to have his head knocked off, and if he kept up with what he was doing, it would be sooner rather than later. Getting back to work, he was nearly finished with the water lines when he realized how late it was getting. Making sure that he locked up his house this time, he made his way to the place he'd been staying for a while now.

The condos in town were the perfect place for him to get what he needed and not have to mess with anyone while he was getting it. From the end of town where he lived, there was little foot traffic and even fewer neighbors. The condos were getting into ill repair, and he'd have to do something about that soon, as he owned them as well, but not today. He wanted his house finished up before he took on any more projects.

~*~

It took him all of an hour to talk to the man about his couch. He'd forgotten that they had changed up the material that it was made from and had to change it back before they'd take it back. He'd not realized that the couch had been broken while they had been on it, and thought that a little roughhousing like they'd done shouldn't have broken two of the legs off. They'd been rough on them, but not that bad.

It had been cleaned up by the sunshine that he'd let into the house, and he was happy that it wasn't as ruined as they thought it had been. After finally getting the man to replace the one that they had, he was going to remember not to recommend the store to any of the others. The man had been rude from the first time he'd picked up the phone and got worse as they spoke. Even if he didn't replace the couch, he should have been nicer about the call. Just as he was hanging up the line, he saw Tabitha. She looked as frustrated as he felt. He asked her what was wrong.

"I just got off the phone with the police department. They're telling me that my mother wants me to bring her some things, and I'm not willing to do it. Not to mention, she wants to talk to me again. I've told them before that I'm not going down there to talk to her about what she wants from me. I guess she has it in her head that she can get what she wants because the judge told her she could. He didn't say any such thing." He held her while she ranted. "Did you know that there's a man in town trying to buy up property? I guess he went out to Rance's place to bother him, and he called the police."

"I'm surprised that he didn't just take care of the man if he's bothering him. Rance isn't one to suffer fools lightly. And he dislikes humans a great deal." She asked about her and Calla. "You've not been human since we met. But no, I believe that he loves the two of you very much. Like a sister to him."

"Good, because I love him as well as the others. They're protective of me, too, and I like that as well." She sat down on the couch that was still in good shape. "Did you have any trouble with the salesman? I could feel your tension all the way home. I hope they'll be able to get us a replacement."

"They're taking care of it tomorrow. We'll just have to remember that we changed out the color and material again so that it matches. He nearly had a cow when I gave him the wrong description of the couch that is broken." He told her how he'd had a little bit of a fit when he said that he'd tried to warn them of the daintiness of the legs. "I don't remember him saying anything like that, and I told him so. We'll have to reinforce them when they get here so that when we have a little fun on them, they don't send us to the floor."

They'd both left the house earlier this morning and hadn't been together at all today. It was the first time that he had not spent the day with her, and he found that he got a great deal done. Not that he didn't miss her, because he had a great deal, but he needed to spend less time with her so that he could keep up on the things that would keep them in money, like his investments. While spending less time with her had been good for things other than them making love all the time, he didn't like leaving her to herself because he missed her.

That sounded harsh even to his ears. Like he'd not wanted to spend any time with her because he was getting nothing done. Well, he wasn't, but he didn't think that was all on her. He'd been the one who wanted to stay home with her. He was going to have to figure out a way to balance out the need to work and the need to be around his mate. It should be easy, as they had the rest of their lives together to figure it out.

As Tabitha ate her dinner, he thought of all the things that needed to be taken care of. He needed an office that he could use that wouldn't be around the house. He knew that if he had to go someplace to work, he'd be better at it, especially with Tabitha having things to do as well. They both had things that needed to be taken care of, and he was going to make sure that they had time to get them done. Even if he had to work from sunup to sundown to get it finished up.

"I was just thinking about having an office too." He asked if she'd read his mind. "No, you mumble when you're upset about something. Anyway, we both need someplace to go during the day so that we're not all over one another all the time. As much as I enjoy having sex with you, we're going to wear each other out before much longer then what will we do? I think that we have just enough sex as it is, but I'm worn out all the time. If we keep this up, we'll need all new furniture again, and that will not make us look good to the salespeople around town."

She had a point. "What do you say we have sex when it's bedtime and nothing more?" She said that she didn't like that, but could see the reason for it. She really needed her sleep. "I'm sorry that I'm keeping you up at night. But I so love the way you make me come when we're playing around."

"I love it too, but seriously, I don't know how much longer I can do this." She looked ready to cry, and he pulled her into his arms. She looked up at him. "Are you mad at me because I want us to slow down a bit? I'm sorry, but I really don't know how much longer I can go without proper sleep."

"I should have thought of that, and that's on me. I didn't think about you not being as strong as I am. We'll be good from now on, so that I don't break you." She smacked him on the chest and laid her head there. "It's been a long time since I've had anyone to love. Perhaps I'm just afraid to lose you or something. I know that you won't leave me, but I have gone so long without anyone meaningful in my life that I've gone a little overboard."

"We both have." She pulled away and began setting things out for dinner. They usually ate in the kitchen on nights that the cook was off, and tonight was no different. She was getting out the stuff to make herself some dinner when he sat down on one of the stools that surrounded the kitchen table. "I discovered something today. I have a lot more magic than I did before. Nothing that I can see a huge use for, but enough that I can will myself from room to room. That's all I've practiced with, is from room to room, but I wonder how far I can go with it. How far can you go when you travel by magic?"

"As far as I want, I guess. I never really gave it any thought. I just want to be someplace, and I use my magic to will myself there." He did think about it then. "I've been to different countries, so I think it's safe to say that I can go anywhere I wish. We'll have to practice to see how far you can go."

"I'd like that. Also, I can touch someone now and tell what they are. The man who's been going around town trying to buy up property is half human and half wolf. I thought there was some rule about having to report to the alpha around the town that you're in." He said he might not know that he's half wolf. "Good point. I didn't know that I had a vampire in my family. How can you find out? He has a bit of magic that he's aware of. I guess that's why I figured that he knew."

"Conri will be able to tell. I'll let him know that one of his kind is causing some trouble and see if he wants anything to do with it. Conri's a good man, and I've heard that he's found his mate. That'll be good for him and his brothers if they start to have their own halves come to them. They're as old as we are." She poured her hot soup into the bowl and got herself some crackers. He noticed that she brought them to herself with magic, and he thought that was wonderful. Sirous watched as she ate a few sips of her hot soup. "I have gone over the banking statements that the banker told me to do. Nothing seems out of the ordinary to me. How about if you have a look with fresh eyes and tell me what it is he sees? He seems to think that we're losing money in a couple of investments. That's normal, I think, but I don't want to get too far behind on them."

"Did I tell you that I got the check from the burin today? It was for quite a bit of money. I had no idea that the man was worth that much." He said that he'd been investing well before he'd been killed, and they'd been surprised by the amount as well. "I'm going to put it in the bank and not touch it. We might want to take a vacation someday, and that will be good for it. Do you have a lot of money?"

"We do have a great deal of money." He watched as she licked her lips free of the soup she was having and had to think about what he'd been saying. "Billions and billions of dollars in cash that is stashed around. Then there is land and homes. We own one in every country. You'll have to remember that I've been around for a long time before cities started to pop up, and I've held onto it throughout the years."

"I do forget about that at times. You don't look older than me, but I know that you are. Brew's mother is even older than you guys are, and I find that hard to believe as well." She finished her dinner and put her bowl and spoon in the sink. "I have a book that I want to finish up if you're finished in here."

"We'll retire to the living room then." As they settled on the couch, he thought about what they'd been talking about earlier about making love so much. He would admit that he wanted her even now, but he was just noticing the dark shadows under her eyes. And her skin was a little pale. He wasn't going to take all the blame, but most of it he could. "Is there anything on the television that you'd like to watch? I will confess that I've not watched it overly much in the last couple of decades. I don't believe that I've even been to a movie house either in that long."

They had a good time running through the stations on it, only to find there was nothing either of them wanted to watch. He'd heard that said before. Hundreds of stations, but nothing you wanted to pause on to watch. Sirous didn't mind turning it off. A book would do him better in the long run.

Just as he was ready to get up and use the bathroom, he noticed that Tabitha had fallen asleep with the book on her chest. He didn't want to move as they were foot to foot on the couch. Just watching her sleep had him feeling guilty again, and he got up without disturbing her. When he returned, she was still resting but in a different position. Covering her up against the chill of the air conditioning, he decided that if she was asleep in an hour, he would take her to their bed and hope that she'd sleep all night. She needed it a great deal.

At eleven-thirty, he'd put Tabitha to bed hours ago; he was finished looking over the paperwork about an investment that he was thinking about investing in. It was something that he had planned on looking over tomorrow, but he had time now and finished it up. He wasn't going to invest in it at this time, but he would keep an eye on it. It had potential, but the company was struggling to make deadlines now, and investing in it would be like pouring money into a pit. Nothing would come of it.

As he made his way up to their bedroom after locking up the house, he thought about how he'd found his mate so easily and hoped it would be the same for the others. He had to believe that she was out there for each of them because if he didn't, all he could think about was how lonely they'd be. Especially Rance and Rutger.

They're parents had died when they were very young, and they'd been raised by another older couple. They didn't have anyone who loved them, not like he and Brew did with their parents, having lived for so long after they were born. If anyone deserved happiness and love, it would be the two of them.

Crawling into bed with Tabitha, she rolled over

to wrap herself around him. She still had not stirred, and he knew then how much she'd needed the rest. After settling down in the covers, he held her to him and waited for sleep to take him. Sometimes he'd be so tired when he went to bed that he couldn't sleep, and tonight seemed to have been one of those nights. He didn't really need to rest as much as his Tabitha did, so he was content to hold her.

"Oh my darling, I love you." He whispered to her gently, then kissed her on her cheek. "You've given me so much, and I fear that I've not given you much in return. I'm going to make it up to you as soon as tomorrow."

The first thing he was going to do was to plan a long vacation for just the two of them. They'd see the world one country at a time and enjoy that for a change. Yes, he thought, that was just what they needed. Time away from the little town and get out into much larger cities where they could be lost to the world.

Before You Go...

HELP AN AUTHOR

write a review

THANK YOU!

Share your voice and help guide other readers to these wonderful books. Even if it's only a line or two, your reviews help readers discover the author's books so they can continue creating stories that you'll love. Log in to your favorite retailer and leave a review. Thank you.

AWARD WINNING, BESTSELLING AUTHOR

Kathi S. Barton is an award-winning and bestselling author known for her steamy paranormal romances and unforgettable characters. A recipient of the prestigious Pinnacle Book Achievement Award, her books have topped the charts on Amazon and All Romance eBooks, earning her a loyal global readership.

Kathi lives in Nashport, Ohio, with her husband, Paul. When she's not crafting passionate love stories set in magical worlds, she enjoys camping, exploring local auctions, and attending county fairs, where Paul showcases his artwork and pottery. Her creative spark—fueled by a muse she describes as a cross between Jimmy Stewart and Hugh Jackman—brings her stories to vivid, heartfelt life.

Paranormal romance with plenty of heat is her favorite genre, and she loves connecting with her readers. Feel free to reach out—Kathi would love to hear from you.
Email: aaronskiss@gmail.com
Blog: kathisbartonauthor.blogspot.com